DRIFTERS' ALLIANCE

BOOK ONE

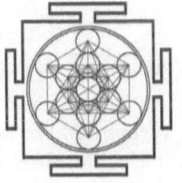

Books by Elle Casey

CONTEMPORARY URBAN FANTASY

War of the Fae (10-book series)
Ten Things You Should Know About Dragons
(short story, The Dragon Chronicles)
My Vampire Summer
Aces High

DYSTOPIAN

Apocalypsis (4-book series)

SCIENCE FICTION

Drifters' Alliance (ongoing series)
Winner Takes All (short story prequel to Drifters'
Alliance, Dark Beyond the Stars Anthology)
The Ivory Tower (short story standalone, Beyond the
Stars: A Planet Too Far Anthology)

ROMANCE

By Degrees
Rebel Wheels (3-book series)
Just One Night (romantic serial)
Just One Week
Love in New York (3-book series)
Shine Not Burn (2-book series)
Bourbon Street Boys (4-book series)
Desperate Measures
Mismatched

ROMANTIC SUSPENSE

*All the Glory: How Jason Bradley Went from
Hero to Zero in Ten Seconds Flat*
Don't Make Me Beautiful
Wrecked (2-book series)

PARANORMAL

Duality (2-book series)
Monkey Business (short story)
Dreampath (short story standalone,
The Telepath Chronicles)
Pocket Full of Sunshine (short story & screenplay)

DRIFTERS' ALLIANCE

BOOK ONE

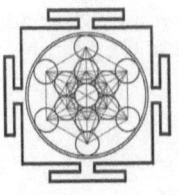

ELLE CASEY

All names, places, and events depicted in this book are fictional and products of the author's imagination.

No part of this publication may be reproduced, stored in a retrieval system, converted to another format, or transmitted in any form without explicit, written permission from the publisher of this work. For information regarding redistribution or to contact the author, write to the publisher at the following address:

Elle Casey

PO Box 14367

N Palm Beach, FL 33408

Website: www.ElleCasey.com

Email: info@ellecasey.com

ISBN/EAN-13: 978-1-93-945561-1

Paperback formatted by Slaven Kovacevic

FIRST EDITION

DEDICATION

To Jef,
otherwise known as Jean-Francois,
my friend who's always up for an adventure.
I would definitely want him on my crew
if I ever found myself in deep space.

CHAPTER ONE

EVERYTHING I'VE WORKED FOR, DREAMED about, studied, and planned…everything I've suffered and sacrificed and paid for with tears and strife. *Everything*, has come to this — a single moment in an underground bar in Centurion 4, the farthest Dark Settlement Station in the Triangulan Galaxy. I'm sitting at a table covered in scars and nicks, its surface stained with the droplets of ten thousand ales and liquors and the occasional splatter of blood. Across from me is the man who has what I want. What I *need*. And I'm not leaving here without it.

My nostrils quiver as the odors coming from the bar and the people surrounding us intrude on my thoughts. *Man, this place stinks like a goatherd's biodome.* I know this from personal experience. Being a grounded drifter at sixteen means when someone has a job that pays credits and includes the occasional meal, you say 'Yes, please', even if it means shoveling goat shit into disposal units all day long.

Sitting across from me is the only man stupid or cocky enough to ante up his drifter ship in a single hand of givit — a smuggler, chancer, and sometimes dirty, rotten thief, otherwise known as Langlade, commander of the Kinsblade fleet. Not bad-looking with that wavy dark hair of his, but not so great either. His nose has been broken about five times too many for him to ever be called hand-some, and he's a little too old for my taste, pushing for-ty-odd Old-Earth years if he's a day.

In the middle of the table is the pot, and the better givit hand takes all: one hand, one winner, that's it. Langlade's anted up the ownership papers to his number three drift-er ship, and I've contributed the only thing I have left of any value: a promissory note offering up my virginity. In a place like this, anyone would be hard pressed to deter-mine which was the more valuable treasure. I'm biased of course, having guarded my precious innocence for a full nineteen years now, but even I'm not sure. I've wanted to captain my own DS for as long as I can remember, and I'm so damn close to that goal right now, I can already taste the vapors running through her lines.

Langlade's lazy voice cuts into my thoughts. "So, what's it going to be, *Cass*, girl of unknown origin, smart enough to play a fair hand, but stupid enough to bet against me? You going to pick a card and call it a night or what?" The cocky bastard looks to his left and right as he rests his elbow on the table, a boastful smile lighting up his dirty, scarred face as he puts on a show for the many onlookers that surround the table. "And when I say 'call it a night', I mean 'get in my bunk', of course."

He turns his attention back to me, his accent growing thicker as he notices my hand resting on the knife I keep next to me at the table. "Better save your energy. You're going to need it, *Lass*."

Bile fills my throat. Bunk in with *him*? Not in this lifetime. I'd rather stab him in the heart and be hung for the crime. I didn't say no a thousand times over to a bunch of really cute guys just to lose my woman's shield to a dog like him.

Raucous laughter flows over my head, but I barely hear it. I've been pretending to care what they think, pretending to be sweating this game, all the while concentrating like an A-Level bore drill navigator. I'm watching for Langlade's tell, the sign that will clue me in to his givit. I know he has one worth taking; he's way too happy right now for me to believe he has nothing in that hand of his. I'm just not sure whether my prize is the card his gaze keeps flicking to or the one his eye avoids.

When his pinky finally moves, twitching over the card he's taking pains not to see, I know. I suddenly *know* with every instinct in my body screaming, *Givit! It's there! Take it from him, now!*

When the dealer taps the table on my side, signaling my turn to choose a card from Langlade's hand, I reach over and pluck the card second from the left, without hesitation— or so it seems to the crowd. But of course I hesitated. It might only have been a fraction of a second, but it was long enough for me to wonder at his question: would I walk away from the table tonight with a DS, a drifter ship to call my own, or would I walk away doomed to a life of selling my body and soul to survive? Because after this game, those are the only two possible outcomes left to me. I've spent every single foodcredit I've ever managed to save to get to this table tonight.

I turn the card over as it reaches my hand and a smile twitches at the corner of my mouth. My heart is almost exploding with relief and the adrenaline that comes from such a win. It's all over but the crying and blood-letting now; there's no way he can beat me, and there's no way he can refuse to hand over the ship. There are too many witnesses, several of whom he does business with who wouldn't allow a guy to live who doesn't pay off his debts owed fair and square.

Tucking the king of hearts in with six other winning cards, I wink at Langlade. "Save your own energy, you ugly sonofabitch, because I'll be sleeping in your bunk *alone* tonight."

"You sure about that?" He lays his cards out, letting each one flick on the table individually so everyone can add them up as they fall.

My heart pounds in my chest so hard it almost feels like it's trying to escape. Then the tally comes together in my head, and I can breathe once again. *Close but not close enough, thank all that the universe holds.*

I place my cards on the table all together, leaving off the dramatic flair displayed by my opponent, and then lean back in my chair with a go-fall-in-a-black-hole smile beaming out from my hot, dusty face. The entire group of scruffs and thieves around us swears and shouts in surprise when they see my hand and realize how thoroughly I've whipped his sorry ass.

"That's a full blockade," I say, winking at the loser across the table. "Aces high."

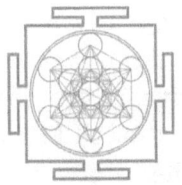

CHAPTER
TWO

I WALK UP THE RAMP to the drifter ship, trying to keep my awe and excitement in check. It wouldn't be cool or smart to reveal my rank amateur status or to gloat over my givit win. Not now. Not when I still need to convince a few of its crew to stay on at least long enough to train their replacements.

Never having actually captained a ship of my own puts me at a terrible disadvantage to every other DS owner in the universe. Sure, I've spent hours and hours in a simulator and read every piece of material available on the fleet, but still … just thinking about the fact that I'm now officially the youngest person to ever own and pilot a ship of this type is enough to make my stomach feel like it's full of eels.

Who's going to stay and fly with me? Who's that stupid or

crazy? Hopefully, at least a handful of people who know what the hell they're doing. I just have to somehow convince them to work for an amateur who has no money to pay their wages. *Ha! Easy! No problem!* It crosses my mind that I might have to give up my virginity anyway to keep the crew happy, even though I've won the ship and I'm literally walking up her entry ramp to take possession. *I wonder if they have a special container for vomit onboard.* I think I'm going to need it.

Most captains have years of experience under their belts before they get to a DS, first on micro transports, light cargo ships, and other of the various smaller craft that share space in the many Triangulum galaxy systems available for travel. But not me. Sure, I've flown two-seaters and a couple fighter rigs, and I've spent a total of a week flying a DS virtually —in bits and pieces whenever I could either pay for the sim time or con someone into letting me use one for free— but mainly I've spent the last three years moving from settlement to settlement as a passenger, catching rides on whatever ships I could. I was never on the flightdeck, always remaining in the hold with everyone else trying to get from one planetary system to the next for the cheapest fare available… or for no fare at all.

I learned early on how to hop rides as an un-manifested stowaway. A girl's gotta do what a girl's gotta do, even if it means sleeping with the dogs or goats or sometimes even the garbage. But not anymore. Not now. No more goats for this girl. From this day forward, I'll be riding on the flightdeck, sitting in the big chair, steering my ship and my future in whatever direction I see fit.

Ugh, the eels are back and they're tying themselves into knots. I rest my hand on my stomach, willing those beasts to calm the hell down.

My tour guide is two paces ahead of me, but his stench is right there under my nose. I don't think this guy's had a single wash in the last five years. His clothing may have started out with color to it, but now his flightsuit is the gray that comes from a build-up of grime I cannot allow myself to think about or I'll never learn where the damn flightdeck is on this thing. I breathe through my mouth as much as possible, but the disturbing thought that I might actually be tasting his stench makes me hold my breath enough to feel lightheaded.

"You ever fly one of these?" he asks, slowing his pace.

I match my steps to his, not at all looking forward to getting that body odor of his any closer. It'll stick in my hair, and then I'll be tempted to cut it all off again. It's taken me three years to get it just past my shoulders where it is now.

"Sure." I shrug as he looks back, acting like it's no big deal to pilot a ship over fifty meters in diameter —fifty point four eight actually, I looked it up— and capable of sustaining speeds faster than anything even close to its size. *And she's all mine, hell yeah!*

"Cuz it ain't no walk in the park, you know. Not when the docks at all the major hubs are at eighty meters and the minors are even less than that."

I swallow past the new lump in my throat. "Just give me the tour," I say, trying to sound confident and tough. Weakness is a liability, especially out here in the badlands, and I've spent a lot of time cultivating my take-no-BS reputation. It would not serve me well to lose it now.

"Sure, no problem," he says. "I'm just sayin'."

"How about instead of doubting my ability to captain *my* ship, you tell me what *you* do on her?" If he says he's the cook, I'm firing him as soon as this tour is over.

I can only imagine what ends up in the food with him in the galley.

He looks over his shoulder, his eyebrow going up. "You mean what I *used* to do on her?"

"Whatever." I shrug, forcing myself not to wilt at his lack of interest in remaining. *If I can't even get Mister Stink-Like-Goatshit to stay, what hope do I have of keeping the rest of them?* And here I thought I'd be deciding whether he stayed or went. *Reality check: Berp, wrong answer.*

"I used to be the pilot," my guide says.

I hesitate as we enter the main cargo hold from the airlock ramp. *Mister Stinkfest piloted this ship?* "But I thought Langlade…"

My tour guide snorts. "Yeah, yeah, I know; you thought Langlade piloted the ship, but you'd be wrong about that." The guy lowers his voice and winks at me. "He couldn't pilot his way out of the Venturion Canyon."

I try not to smile, but it's impossible. If Langlade heard this guy say that he couldn't maneuver a DS in a canyon three kilometers wide and known as the perfect practice ground for teaching children how to pilot personal ground craft, my guide would probably be missing a finger for the insult. Maybe more than one.

Langlade has such a wild reputation in the settlements, it's impossible to separate fact from fiction. My own story of winning this ship away from him will definitely go down in history as one of those myths too crazy to be believed. Did it really happen? Did he really lose his ship to a nineteen year old girl in a single hand of givit? Betting his ship against her innocence? Some people will believe it; Langlade is just that kind of guy.

Now that I know he sucks at piloting a DS, though, I'm curious about some of the other rumors swirling around his reputation. "I heard he once evaded capture through the exhaust tunnels over at the Transad Volcano system."

"Myth. Ain't nobody that crazy, not even him."

"That he slept with the daughter of Andromeda System's high commander?"

The guy smiles, as if a happy memory just sailed through his mind. "Ahhh, now *that* one is true. I remember hightailing it out of there in my skivvies." He looks at me and loses his smile, frowning in disappointment. "No more of that'll be going on now, I guess."

"What?" I snort, hoping I misunderstand. "You guys running around working in your birthday suits? No thanks." I shudder for effect. And then I actually picture him unzipping that flight suit and shudder in real disgust. *Please, no. Never, ever. Not on my watch.*

He winks at me, making my stomach churn even more. I say the first thing that comes to mind. "If you don't quit looking at me like that I'm going to stab you in the eyeball."

He leans back and barks out a laugh so loud it makes me jump.

My hand goes to my chest as my heart races. Then I scowl when I realize how girly that made me look. "Crazy bastard," I mumble.

He's still smiling. "Birthday suits. Why not? It does get hot in here sometimes." He continues on, pointing to a panel on the wall glowing with different colored switches and buttons. "That's your docking panel." He's back to being serious. "You can go manual down here or work it from the flightdeck. Sometimes it's a bit futzy, so I recommend you position someone down here, just in case."

"What? Futzy?" I walk by it as he cuts off down a hallway. "What do you mean?" I stare at the panel, wondering what the hell is going on with this thing. *Is it broken? Are all DSs like this?* I never used the simulator to run the more mundane systems on the DS; opening cargo doors and flushing filtration systems were too boring to waste sim time on, or so I thought. Now I'm thinking I should have spent some of my hours on something other than flying. To my credit, though, I did start to max out the Skill Levels on my last few sessions. Hopefully that means I'll be able to get the damn thing out of here and into the Dark without damaging her hull. *There's gotta be someone who'll stay on who knows how to dock this ship, right?*

"I mean what I said." His response to my question bounces around the metal walls, floors, and ceilings.

"You said it's futzy." I jog to catch up with him.

"Yeah. She's an old ship. That means futzy electronics and such. You'll figure out her quirks once you've flown a few million light years on her." He turns around and walks backward. "Just better keep it local until you do. You wouldn't want to learn about her non-spark problem halfway to Andromeda, now would ya?"

My face blanches as I imagine being adrift in the middle of nowhere without a gravity field holding me to the floors, slowly turning into a jellyfish as my bones disintegrate. But I manage to answer with false confidence anyway. "Probably not."

He walks normally again, laughing to himself. "Probably not," he mocks, shaking his head. "Oh, this is going to be one for the record books, all right."

I steel myself against his condescension. Leaving home at sixteen and surviving these three, long years on the outskirts of civilization, crawling and fighting my way to get to where I am today... that ain't nothin'. I'll overcome this obstacle just like I have all the others, and in the meantime, I'll pretend like I know what the hell I'm doing. *What's the worst that could happen, anyway?* I could die in a massive explosion and turn into a wisp of smoke in less than a second. At least it'd be a quick death.

"How old are you anyway?" he asks, stopping just outside a metal door with a round spinning lock on its surface.

"Old enough."

"Old enough to play cards. But are you old enough to pilot this ship? Manage a crew of ten men who go long stretches without seeing a real woman? Feed that many mouths? How you gonna pay for food and basic supplies?"

I look at the door next to my tour guide and lift my chin, ignoring the dread that wants to fill me full of darkness. "What's behind that door?"

"Engine room."

I nod once. "Let's see it."

"You gonna answer my question?"

I glare at him, staring deep into his muddy brown eyes. They look as dirty as the rest of him. "You gonna get on with my tour? Because I don't have all day."

He shrugs, and rotates the airlock wheel, shoving the heavy door into the wall pocket with the help of his shoulder once it's free of its locking mechanism. "Suit yourself."

I walk into the dark space, inhaling the scent of warm machinery and buzzing circuitry, smiling as I realize that all of this glorious metal and polymer is mine. Every last stinking bolt and burning fuse has my name on it. My pride lasts all of about three seconds before a strange odor intrudes on my thoughts and something that looks out of place catches my eye. *Is that smoke I see by that panel over there?*

A noise off to my right pulls my attention away from the panel and the smoke. My eyes widen as the maker of that sound comes into view. Before I can think to keep my thoughts to myself, the words are coming out of my mouth.

"Holy shit, you're a ginger." I've never seen a real one in my entire life, although I'd heard stories about them: hair as orange as coppura wire, spots of dark color on their faces and arms, teeth yellow like a desert yew flower.

He holds out his hand and smiles. "Yes, indeed. Gus is the name. And you are...?"

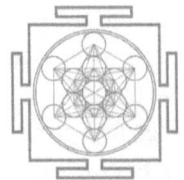

CHAPTER
THREE

GUS SMILES, HIS TEETH GLOWING in the dark-ened room. They're not nearly as yellow as the myths would have had me believe.

"Cass Kennedy," I say, taking his hand in mine, grip-ping it like my father taught me an eon ago. 'The power play starts at the introduction,' he'd say.

I can't believe there's a ginger working on my ship. I'm trying not to stare at the spots on his face, remnants of Earthbound DNA that have been otherwise rubbed out through medical interventions over two centuries. *Be cool. Don't be a ginger-freak.* I gaze around the room as our hands drift apart, taking in the wall of computers, the machines churning and humming, and the table to my right full of random parts and circuitry. The smoke has dissipated, making me think I imagined it. "You in charge here?"

"Sure am."

I can feel his eyes roaming over my body, but each time I look directly at him, his attention shifts to the ceiling or the floor. I'm used to the attention, but I always ignore it. I decided long ago to trade on my intelligence and not any sort of feminine wiles I might have buried deep down inside, figuring the former to be more reliable and longer-lasting anyway. Besides, I was never much for flirting. Whenever I've tried, it's come out awkward and uncomfortable for everyone involved.

Instead, I've learned to stick with the things I'm good at, namely: playing givit, fighting —old school hand-to-hand combat being my favorite style—, reading people's unspoken thoughts and using them to my advantage, and pushing toward my goal of captaining my own DS. What can I say? I'm not a very complicated girl; what you see is what you get with Cass Kennedy. I wear my knife on my leg so no one can claim surprise when they feel its blade.

"Like hell he's in charge." Another voice comes from behind the first, and a second glowing smile and shock of orange hair comes out of the darkness. "I'm chief here, not him." He holds out his hand, ignoring my look of surprise at finding not just one ginger, but two, living on the ship, each a copy of the other. "I'm Tam, head engineer, nice to meet you."

Gus elbows him in the ribs. "*Mechanics* engineer. Not electronics." He winks at me. "That's me. Head *electronics* engineer."

"Clones," I say without thinking. First gingers and then clones. Of course; it makes complete sense now. I'm only a little disappointed to find out this isn't the universe's work in front of me. All those years of the OSG's careful DNA monitoring and attention to family lineage to keep the human race as pure as possible has had some negative effects — like no more gingers for us to stare at.

Gus scowls, while Tam leans over to spit on the floor.

"Clones?" Tam says, practically snarling. "Hell no, we ain't no clones."

Gus chimes in. "We're *au naturel*. Check it." He lifts his chin, keeping his eyes on me. His voice changes with the stretching of his throat. "See?"

I look for the telltale blue cloning mark and see nothing but a guy who really should check the creases of his neck for dirt once in a while. *Flaming dwarf stars, have mercy. Don't they have water on this ship?*

"What?" he asks, catching my expression. "What's wrong?"

Tam looks at his brother's neck and laughs. "You could have a tattoo of a fucking warship on your gullet and she'd never see it, you're so damn dirty. Why don't you take a shower once in a while?"

Gus flicks his brother with his rag, making it snap against his bare arm. "Why don't you fix the fucking filter so I *can* take a shower, dick?"

I bite my lip to keep from laughing out loud, worried if I join in with the game they'll think less of me. A captain has to be serious and above stupid conversations about taking showers if she wants to have the crew's respect, and I really need to keep these guys onboard with me if at all possible. The friends who've committed to following me in this grand scheme have no training for running an engine room, and a DS is only as good as its engineers, that's a fact. Without these two gingers or someone with their skills onboard, my DS will be just a floating tub of junk worth less than the crud under my fingernails.

I take a quick look at my hands. *Ew. There really is a lot of crud under there. I should probably stop judging the creases in Gus's neck. Or was it Tam's neck?* I look up and realize I cannot tell them apart. Just then, the reason for the dirty neck hits me.

"There's a problem with the water filtration?" I look from one engineer to the other, waiting for an explanation. This could be a big issue, one that could keep us at this station for much longer than I'd planned. Water filtration hangups usually indicate a problem with the hydrothrusters, and even more alarming, the available water supply. Without fresh water, both crews and their biosystems die. Water flowing freely and properly for all systems is the number one priority on any DS that means to actually function as a drifter's home. *Holy shit, what have I gotten myself into?*

"Not too big a problem," Gus says —or the one I think is Gus— smiling much harder than he should. "Just need a few parts is all."

"I hope you brought a bucket of credits with you," Tam says, shaking his head slowly, "cuz we have a list a mile long of parts we need."

"Parts you *want*, not need," my tour guide says, annoyed, stepping back into the corridor.

I look from the twins to my guide, remembering my entrance minutes earlier. The gruff old guy turned the handle to not just open the door, but to unlock it. I turn to face him. "Wait a minute … you shut them in here and *lock* it?"

The guide shrugs, like it's no big deal to lock crewmen inside a dark room all day and night. "Captain's orders. Everyone who's on duty, stays on duty." He glares at the twins. "Some people have a tendency to stray when we're docked, otherwise."

The twins look at me, their faces the picture of innocence as they speak simultaneously. "We have no idea what he's talking about."

"Come on, Captain," the guide says, gesturing down the corridor. "I have a meeting with a whore that starts in about an hour, and I don't want to be late." He walks away, leaving me in the doorway to the engine room feeling slightly queasy.

"Lucky girl, that whore," Gus says with exaggerated wistfulness, his eyes following the man as he clomps away, his heavy boots clanging on the metal grate flooring.

I imagine that bow-legged, smelly, scarred-up old man standing in the middle of my bedroom, stark naked with expectations of sex, and simultaneously realize how close I came to sharing his whore's fate today in that hand of givit.

My fingers go to my lips and press. I talk around them. "Oh, God, I think I just vomited in my mouth a little." I can't stop looking at the hunch-backed figure of the man who will soon be paying a ton of money for sex, because that's the only way he'd get anyone to accommodate his needs.

"Awesome." Tam starts tucking in his shirt like he's suddenly in a big hurry. "Well, Captain Whatever-Your-Name-Is, it was nice meeting you, but I'm outta here." He glances at the disappearing form of my guide and then grins at me as he steps out into the corridor. He's centimeters away; I can smell the odor of ship mechanics on him, and it's not entirely unpleasant. Obviously, I've been dreaming about owning a DS for way too long.

"Where are you going?" I ask as his brother Gus steps out into the corridor to join his twin and licks his fingers, using his spit to slick his crazy red hair down.

"Into the station," Gus responds, buttoning the top of his work shirt. "Gotta find a job. How do I look?" He grins as he waits for my reaction to his hasty ministrations.

I have no idea what to say in response. His hair looks like it was washed two weeks ago, dried behind a DS thruster, and spritzed with a coating of pig oil.

"Uh… fine?"

He starts to walk away, but I grab the sleeve of his shirt. "Wait! Stay. Don't go look for another job."

Gus looks down at my hand and then up at my face. "You got money to pay wages?"

"I've got something better than that." I lift my chin, hoping he won't notice I'm shaking a little over that slight fib.

His eyes widen and then begin to roam over my body again, only this time he's not trying to hide his interest.

I glare at him, ready for battle. "Not that, idiot." If he even thinks about laying a finger on me, I will cut him to the bone, and it's better he knows that right up front.

He smiles briefly, maybe a little ashamed. "Oh. Sorry." He cringes as the next words come out of his mouth. "But honestly, that's the only thing I know of that's better than straight up gencredits or foodcredits. No offense to your ladyness or whatever."

"Forget that shit," I say brushing off his awkward apology. "I'm talking about something much more valuable than credits. More long-lasting. I'm talking about *freedom*." The fire in my belly lends a fervor to my words that I feel with every nanogram of my soul. I've been dreaming of this event for so long, it's engraved in my mind. I know exactly how it needs to happen and how to get to my destination. I just need like-minded people to buy into my vision and help me. This is a journey that cannot be taken alone.

The brothers exchange looks.

"Freedom?" Tam asks.

"Tell us more," Gus says, moving to stand shoulder to shoulder with his twin.

My words come out in a rush. "Stay and work as engineers for me, and together we drift. We do our own thing." I nod at the heavy steel entrance to the engine room. "And your door stays unlocked."

"But what about sex?" Gus asks. "Because if I don't get to a settlement once in a while, I…"

Tam punches him in the back. "Shut up, dick, just listen to her." He drops his voice and speaks softly out of the side of his mouth. His gaze is fixed on me but his words are for his brother. "It's time to negotiate."

Gus nods slowly, his eyes narrowing. "Yeah, riiight. Okay." He turns his attention to me, his grin back in place, but this time, it's decidedly sharp. "What else besides freedom and the drifting stuff?"

I shrug, trying to calm my racing pulse through sheer power of will. "What else do you want?" *Anything but sex or money. Say anything but sex or money, and I'll find a way to make it work.*

"A take," Tam says in a rush, "of whatever you bring on board. To do with what we want."

Boom, goes success. I just got my hands on his givit, *yeah baby.*

I fight to keep the smile off my face. "What if I take cargo for transport to outer settlements?" I clamp my teeth down on the inside of my cheek waiting for his answer.

"Why would you want to do that?" Gus asks, bewildered.

Tam nudges him, but keeps his attention on me. "We'll take a percentage of the transport fee."

"What if it's hard goods for sale?" I'm definitely warming to the idea of a split. This could make my complete lack of funds a non-issue, or at least less of one. Not that I have any cargo or goods to sell or anything else, but I can get some. I know I can. I have friends, I have connections, and I have desperation, which is a pretty powerful thing in the hands of this girl.

"If you have hard goods, we could take a share and do what we want with it. Sell it, use it." Tam shrugs. "It would be ours."

Gus points at me, sounding tough for the first time since I met him. "And no take-backs. Blood contract. Nothing less."

"You coming or not?!" my guide yells from around the corner.

"We'll discuss the percentage when you get back," I say in a low voice. "I have to finish the tour and get the keycodes. Don't be late. We take off in two hours at zero three hundred."

Gus and Tam exchange looks and devious smiles.

"She thinks she's getting keycodes," Gus says.

"Silly little girl," Tam says.

Less than a second after that last word leaves his mouth, I have Tam shoved up against the wall with my knife at his throat. My blood is boiling in my veins, and I'm completely committed to the idea of spilling some of his. He's just found one of my hot buttons and pressed it, poor guy.

He looks down at me with surprise and fear in his eyes. "Uhhh…"

"Don't ever call me that again." I growl my words so softly only he can hear. *Silly little girl.* I haven't had the luxury of being one of those since I was two years old.

That's when my world changed forever and I was forced to become something else entirely.

"Ohhhh kaaaaay." Tam's trying to smile, but failing miserably. "Noted."

Gus looks away to hide his grin.

Sheathing my dagger at my thigh, I leave the gingers to their business. Gus's peals of laughter follow behind me, but I ignore him. Better that they know right from the start that I'm a crazy bitch who's a little sensitive about certain kinds of name calling. That way, when they sign their blood contract with me, they won't be able to back out later crying foul.

CHAPTER FOUR

"SO THAT'S IT," THE SMELLY tour guide says. "You've seen most of her. And it's time for me to go, so…"

"Just one more thing," I say, hoping the little bit of information I gleaned over the years about the DS fleet from my study materials and fellow bar patrons was correct. "The keycodes."

He keeps walking, heading for the door that will take him from the flightdeck out into the corridors that lead to the dock and his date with a woman I will personally send up a prayer for as soon as he's gone.

"Ain't no keycodes for this DS," he says.

Is that normal? Is my information outdated? I have no way of knowing. Dammit, I hate being such a damn gloob at all this.

"Why not?" I shout at his back, hoping I'm not revealing my complete incompetence.

"Because you got them crazy gingers on board, that's why."

And then he's gone. No more tour guide, no more information, no more stink. I take a whiff of air and scowl. *Okay, so there's still some stink left behind.* I need to put this ship on a vacuum cycle for about three hours to clear it out, assuming its vacuum system even works.

I turn around and stare out the clearpanels of my new ship, not quite believing it's real. *Did I really win this baby in a card game or did I dream the entire thing?* Beyond the clearpanels there are men and women walking around inside the dockside pedestrian tunnels, some of them working and others just loitering. It's impossible to tell who is doing which, because so many of the dockside transactions are done with gestures, a look, or a predetermined sign of some sort.

A lot of effort goes into avoiding the heavy tariff loads assessed by the Omega System Group. The OSG is omnipresent, but spread thin enough that a lot can slip through the cracks if you know what you're doing and have the right connections. These are things, places, and relationships that I've been cultivating for a long while now, and it's all about to pay off. The smile I've been fighting all day comes out to be shared with no one. I'm alone now; I can afford to be weak.

My joy lasts all of about five seconds. When I recognize the figure of Langlade striding through one of the clear pedestrian tunnels toward my ship's dock, my entire body goes on tense alert. The panel of buttons and touchscreens before me swims and blurs. *Which one was it that closed the main airlock?* My tour guide may have mentioned it, but he was in such a hurry to get to his sex-date, it was kind of hard to group his rushed words into comprehensible sentences.

"Need a hand?" asks someone from behind me.

I spin around, my hand going to the dagger at my thigh. *I'm slipping. How did he sneak up on me so easily?* My heart is pounding hard enough to flutter the black, two-part, second-skin flightsuit I'm wearing.

An older man of sixty or so years, dark-skinned and white-afro-haired, smiles at me, his brown-stained teeth reminding me of the men I know to inhale smokeplant as a habit. His light-colored, loose-fitting pants and long tunic are about as non-threatening as a uniform can be, helping me to relax. When I am killed one day, it won't be by a man wearing linen.

"Perhaps I can be of service," he says.

I walk down two steps to reach his level and hold out my hand. "Cass. New captain."

He takes my cool fingers in his warm ones and grips lightly. "Jeffers Melville, at your service." He gives a slight bow after our hands slide apart.

Finding myself off-center in his presence, I fold my arms across my chest. He reminds me of my grandfather —a man I respected and sorely miss— and yet, at the same time, this guy moves like a warrior, swift and silent, with a confident air that comes only after a lot of training. I'm not wary enough to draw my weapon, but I'm not leaving myself exposed either.

"And what exactly do you do around here?" I ask, using a tone of voice I imagine a captain would with his crew: strong, respectful, but not inviting any meaningless pleasantries.

His mouth turns down as he considers his answer. "Bit o' this, bit o' that." His hands rest behind him, a military gesture that mirrors the one my father used often, partic-ularly when he was drilling me about what I had done versus what I *should* have done.

My eyebrow goes up, waiting for the real answer to my question. Two can play at this game, but only one person can win. *Aaaand that'll be me.*

His smile is slow in coming, but when it does, it chang-es his whole face. What were sad folds become creases that bear witness to a well-shared, sunny disposition. His ears go back and his entire head of hair lifts; it's like he's become another person entirely. He shrugs, his hands drifting forward to hang by his sides. "I cook, I clean, I medicate. I tend to wounds both seen and unseen."

"So, you're a healer and a domesticant." *A strange com-bination. Maybe Langlade was thrifty or something, asking his crew to double-up on their duties.*

"I'm many things." He looks out the clearpanel, and I follow his gaze just in time to see Langlade disappear from view, getting ever closer to the ship's airlock ramp.

"I am sometimes a person who offers counsel to those in need," he says mysteriously.

When I look back at him, he nods once slowly, never breaking eye contact.

"And I'm in need?" I ask, just to be sure I understand.

"If you consider the fact that the man you practically stole this ship from is about to come aboard, then perhaps yes, you would be. If I were you, I'd press that blue button right there." He nods again, this time toward the control array to my right.

"This one?" My finger hovers over the one I think he means. The word 'CLOSEDOOR' glows on its surface. *Duh. Probably should have noticed that one on your own, Genius.*

He nods.

A second after I press it, a rumbling starts from somewhere deep in the belly of the ship, followed shortly by some muffled shouting. I'm pretty sure it's Langlade and he's watching the door close in his face. Two seconds later, the faint sound is cut off and the rumbling stops.

"Thanks for the advice." I grace Jeffers with one of my rare smiles.

He makes a half bow and then once again fixes his gaze on me. "Have you made your decision about who you're keeping and who you're letting go?"

Is this is a trick question? Can't he see that I'm a complete brownshins at this captaining gig? Maybe not. Maybe I can fake it until I make it, if I can keep the crew members like him on board. "I'd like to keep anyone who wants to stay. I can't pay much, but…"

He waves his hand. "The Kinsblade 3 is my home. If you'll have me, I'll stay."

"Her name's Anarchy." My chin goes up in expectation of his criticism. It may be childish, but I picked that name three years ago, and I haven't thought of another one since. It's perfect. It fits my life and my personal beliefs better than any other name I could come up with.

Another half bow comes. "As you wish."

I sigh loudly, not sure that what I want to say is the right thing, but knowing I'm going to say it anyway. "I really wish you'd stop bowing at me."

"You're the captain, and the captain deserves my respect."

"Can you respect me without the bowing?" I hate that I sound so weak, but something about this old man makes me feel like I'm ten again. And ten-year-olds cannot possibly pilot drifter ships. Hell, nineteen-year-olds can't pilot drifter ships. *Who in the hell do I think I'm fooling?*

He smiles, his eyes twinkling. "I suppose I could manage it. Would you like a cup of tea?"

Disarmed again, I relax. Here I am stressing out about being old enough to own a DS, and all he's worried about are hot drinks. Then his words hit me.

"You have tea here?" I can't imagine how that could be possible. Trading for tea is big business and highly regulated. That the OSG would let Langlade be a party to that network is kind of hard to believe, and it's not like he's the type to be having personal tea parties. *Another mystery aboard the DS Anarchy.*

"We have some plants and herbs. I take it your tour did not include the biogrid?"

"No." I shake my head, afraid to hope for too much. "I just saw the engine room, the cargo hold, a couple of the bunks, and the flightdeck." *A biogrid on a DS? He can't mean what I'm imagining.*

It seems as if my keycode *and* biogrid information is outdated. Not surprising, considering the sources of the DS details I had at my disposal. Men and women who spend most of their lives sitting at the givit tables aren't well known for their honesty or worldliness.

"Tremblay must have been the one to show you around."

Tremblay, aka, Mister Stinkbomb. "He doesn't like tea?"

"More like he was never one to care about where his food comes from, so he wasn't really aware of what was going on in the outer chambers." He gestures toward the door, his voice going deeper. "I think your next stop should be the biogrid. Lucinda will be very pleased to meet you, I'm sure."

"Lucinda?" I walk two paces in front of him off the flightdeck and out into a corridor I've not yet seen. They all look mostly the same, though— gray, gritty, scratched, and in need of some attention.

"Yes. Lucinda's our horticulturist, and, until you came along, the only female onboard."

"Poor girl," I say, wondering how this Lucinda person was able to fend off the advances of her crewmates… or if she even did.

"She managed."

Jeffers' answer leaves more things unspoken than said, making me anxious to meet this woman who somehow grows forbidden tea leaves and lives in the outer chambers of a DS, the area most often used for storage or housing captives, according to my research.

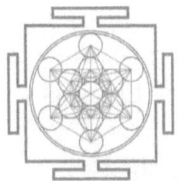

CHAPTER FIVE

THE HORRIBLE STENCH OF ROTTING flesh and acrid poisons hits me as soon as I enter the biogrid chamber. I back up a step, hitting the edge of the entry portal. My hand flies up to my face, and my eyes dart left and right, searching for a mask that will protect my lungs.

"Lucinda, it's me and our new captain," Jeffers says, reaching over and tapping in some numbers and letters into a keypad near the entrance. He seems completely unconcerned about the damage to his lung tissue. The door slides shut, nearly catching my shoulder, and a light goes on above us. I glance up to see its strange blue-green orb glowing from a seam in the wall.

A girl not much older than I am if her skin is anything to judge by comes out from behind the black panel and stops, staring at us. "What's this?" she asks. She doesn't sound happy.

"*This* is our new captain." Jeffers gestures at his crew-mate. "Cass Kennedy, meet Lucinda."

Lucinda blinks a few times as she continues to stare at me. "She's young."

He nods once. "Yes, she is."

"I expected her to be older."

I have the strangest sensation that there's something else going on here besides just an introduction. Assuming I'll figure out what it is soon enough, I step forward, holding out my hand. "Pleasure to meet you, Lucinda."

Lucinda looks to Jeffers, one eyebrow slightly arched. "Polite, too."

My hand continues to hang in the air between us.

Her gaze shifts down to my offer of greeting. "How do I know you mean us no harm?"

I can respect a girl who sticks up for herself and guards her privacy, so I don't let her attitude put me off. But at the same time, she needs to know who the boss is in the room, and I've got news for her. *It ain't the horticulturist.*

I give her a tight smile. "The first step is to shake my hand and say hello. Play nice and up your chances of getting on my good side."

The back corners of her jaws bounce out, but then she takes my hand. Her palm is rougher in comparison to mine, which is surprising; I thought I had bad calluses.

"Hello." Her voice is tone dead.

I have no idea why she's being so bitchy, but I don't care. This is my ship now, and she needs to accept that. Letting her hand go, I sidestep to my right, looking up to the ceiling at the pipes above our heads that are traveling all over in a maze of directions.

"It stinks in here." I shift my gaze to Lucinda just in time to see a tiny smile appear before it disappears again in a flash.

"That's a biosystem for you," she says, shrugging.

"That's funny," I say, trying to act casual, "the bio-domes I worked in never smelled like this."

"You've worked in a biodome?" The implication in her tone is impossible to miss: she doesn't believe me, maybe because I'm missing the telltale brown-stained shins that many of those workers have.

"Yep, I've worked in *two* biodomes, as a matter of fact, and they always smelled of … earth." The word is like magic to me. There is no other scent like the loam of our ancestors' old world, traded like precious metals here in our time. Superstition says that only with some of it added to your biosystem will you ever have a crop worth harvesting.

"Luce, I think we should…"

Jeffers' statement is cut off by Lucinda walking over to halt my further progress into the chamber. "Is there any-thing in particular you'd like to know about our work?" She positions herself in front of a door with a light over it. The light is red.

I nod, pointing at the closed portal behind her. "Yeah. I'd like to know what's behind that door."

She shrugs. "Nothing. Just some noxious weeds. Meat-eating variety. We're doing experiments with them. That's what you smell in here. The off-gasses. Highly toxic if you come into direct contact."

"Really." I don't believe a word coming out of this girl's mouth. I can spot a liar from fifty paces; it's a special talent of mine. It's how I got so good at givit and survived out in the Dark as long as I have.

Reaching past her, I sweep my hand over the lock screen, but nothing happens. I grab the handle and pull. Nothing happens again.

"It's locked," she says. "For crew safety."

Pulling myself up to my full one point six meters, I fix her with a look. My voice is soft, but my tone promises trouble if she doesn't comply. "I'm the captain of this ship, and I have access to every square centimeter of it, seeing as how she's *mine*. What's the code to enter?" Sliding the cover to the keypad away, my fingers hover over the letters and numbers glowing out from the touchscreen, ready to input the sequence she gives me.

"There is no code. It's programmed for biowaves. Only Jeffers and I are permitted entry. It's not safe for anyone else." Her expression displays neither fear nor respect, which only pisses me off more. She's just not getting this at all.

I give her a smile I hope will disarm her. "Not even your former captain?" I find it very hard to believe that Langlade didn't care to know about the crazy experiments that were taking place inside the walls of his hull. Something very strange is going on here.

Her chin goes up in defiance. "No. He was never interested in what we did up here, so long as he had his food and medicines when he needed them."

I shrug casually, even though I feel anything but relaxed. "Regardless, you'll be adding a third biowave to the list of authorized entrants. *Mine.* In the meantime, use yours." I nod at the keypad.

"I don't think that's a good idea." She shakes her head and crosses her arms over her chest.

Okay, play time is over. I don't have time for this shit with Langlade out there on the dock making noise. *Time to turn up the heat.* I take a step closer and slowly slide my dagger from the sheath. It's up next to her face before she even knows my intentions.

"Okay, sweetness, let me be perfectly clear, so we don't get off on the wrong foot with you thinking you run the show up here and that I'm some sort of idiot like Langlade who lets his crew do whatever the hell they please without his even knowing." I flick my gaze to the keypad and then back to her. "Either you open that door for me willingly, or I knock your ass out and open the door with your limp body myself. You might think obeying me is a choice, and you'd be right. It *is* a choice." I press harder against her throat. "Either make the right one now yourself or I'll make the right one for you."

She's shaking and now struggling to breathe too, but it doesn't keep her from answering. "You don't know which part of my body it is."

I grin evilly, loving the fact that she's a crazy bitch too. Too bad there's no one here crazier than me. "I'll start with your forehead and work my way down."

"Okay, that's enough," Jeffers says with a sigh from behind me. He walks over to the door, puts the heel of his palm on the pad, and the door unlocks with a click and a whoosh as it slides into its pocket in the wall.

"Jeffers! No!" Lucinda cries, shoving past me, heedless of the knife just inches from her face. She stops in the open doorway and opens her arms. "No! You can't enter. There's poison in here and things that will steal the breath from your lungs." Her hand fumbles on the wall just inside the door and she comes out with a breather mask, holding it out for me to see before pressing it to her face.

I look from her to Jeffers. There's shock on one face and resignation on another.

"If you never take a risk, you never reap the reward," he says to her.

"If you never take a risk, you never lose anything either," she says to him, tears in her eyes. The mask falls from her face in defeat as her hand drops to her side.

I'm about to ask them what the hell is going on when something hits me: a scent — one that can't have anything to do with poisons or things bad for my lungs. The odor of herbs and water washes over me first. Then something even more amazing: the perfume that can only come from real flowers. A distant memory from my childhood informs my conscious mind of what I'm sensing, but without it, I wouldn't have a single clue what was going on. Flowers are reserved for the Haves, not the Havenots, and Langlade is definitely a member of the latter group, as am I. As of three years ago, in fact.

I slide my knife back home in its sheath and step forward, anxious to confirm my suspicions. "It's Eden," I say, my voice barely above a plain breath. There are stories about places where green things grow in the earth — everything a person could need coming right from the soil at their feet— but I always assumed it was another myth, like the stories of winged dragons and nations where people actually voted for their leaders.

Lucinda's gaze darts in Jeffers' direction and then back toward me. I see conflict in her eyes, a battle between fear and hope reflected with no clear winner. I suddenly know what I have to do.

"I'm not going to hurt your plants. I just want to see what you're growing. I smell … flowers."

"She already knows about the tea," Jeffers says.

Lucinda's entire body sags at that news, her shoulders rounding down and her expression falling into sadness.

"Why?" Her tone has gone weak. Defeated. "Why didn't you talk to me first? Wait and see what she was about first? She could be anybody. She could be with the OSG."

"Not in a million years," I say with disgust.

"Sometimes we just have to have faith that the universe is providing and not taking away." Jeffers gestures with one arm out, the extra width of his sleeves falling toward the floor. "Please, Captain. After you."

As I step into the entrance, Lucinda looks to Jeffers with anger shining out from behind her eyes. "You'd better be right, Healer, or we're all screwed."

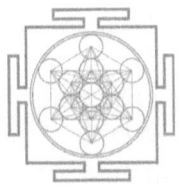

CHAPTER SIX

THE SCENTS INTENSIFY AS I move farther into the chamber, but without light to see by, I have no idea what's creating this unique atmosphere.

No sooner is the thought floating through my mind than a blue-green glow begins to flicker above me. I lift my eyes to the top of the ship's hull, or what I expect to be the top of it, and instead I find myself looking at pipes. And towers. Towers with things protruding from every part of their rounded sides.

"What in the bottom of a black hole…?"

"Biotowers," Jeffers says, appearing at my right shoulder. "Floor to ceiling. All hydroponic."

"But I smelled…"

"Soil?" He smiles. "We do have some things growing in that medium. Some plants that are a little too big to do well without."

Lucinda's voice comes from behind us. "Why don't you go ahead and give her the full tour? Might as well."

Do I detect a hint of pride in her voice? Hmmm, I do believe I do.

"No," I say firmly, my eyes still roaming the ceiling and the intricate maze of pipes. "I want *you* to show me."

"I'm not your servant. Just because I work on this ship doesn't mean I answer to you."

I turn around and smile at her, half laughing at her show of bravado. "Sure it does. Come on. Show me what you've done. I'm interested."

She sniffs, not moving, looking away from me to stare at the wall next to her.

"Fine. I'll show myself around." I stride off down the corridor formed by several growing towers lined up side by side. When I see something that looks a little darker than the other things near it, I take a right turn, losing myself in the leaves around me.

"Don't go down there!" she shouts from behind me.

Good, I'm on the right track. I keep going until I get to a strong scent of mint and turn left. A different glow and the sounds of spraying liquid drive me right and then left again. Eventually I find myself staring at a high stack of rafts floating in square bins of water as long and wide as me. Maybe bigger.

I pull off a leaf, rub it between my fingers and bring it to my nose. "Coriander," I say softly to myself. I lick away the smears from my finger and thumb, bringing a taste I haven't had on my tongue in at least five years. I can't help but smile as I realize how much of the stuff is growing here. And if I'm not mistaken, there are at least four other herbs I learned about in my father's kitchens many years ago, floating on other rafts down the line.

Holy shit. They have a gold mine in here, and Langlade didn't even have a clue.

I start laughing and can't stop. First Jeffers and then Lucinda show up, both of them just staring at me. At least Jeffers smiles in response. Lucinda, on the other hand, just gets more annoyed.

"I don't see what's so funny."

I finally calm down enough to sigh and respond. "What's so funny is you pumping the smells of that shit into the antechamber so none of those droid-heads would want to investigate any farther into your world. Genius." I stand up straighter, losing my smile. "And devious. What have you been doing with the harvest?" I jerk my thumb over at the herbs. "You have herbs, you have tea... I suspect you have just about every vegetable a human would want to eat and maybe even some fruit. How many credits have you stolen from Langlade over the years?"

"We aren't thieves!" Lucinda says, taking a step toward me.

Jeffers' arm going across her middle stops her in her tracks. Lucky for her, he decided to play savior again, because I'm about out of patience with her and her shitty attitude. She needs to step in line or she's off this ship tonight. I don't have time for mutiny, and jobless biogridders are easy enough to find.

"Allow me to explain," he says. "Would you like to see the rest of it as I do that?"

I nod, refusing to play too nice. He might be like my old grandpa, but that's not going to influence how I view their actions. I will, however, withhold judgment until I hear the entire story. I've been known to skirt the edge between right and wrong in the name of survival more than a few times; I can hardly punish others for doing the same. So long as they have a decent reason for doing what they've done, I can be fair.

Jeffers walks and I motion for Lucinda to follow him. I'm not having that wench at my back anytime soon.

She follows my orders for the first time since I met her, but not happily. She scowls as she takes up her position just in front of me.

"We've been working on the infrastructure for this grow chamber for nearly a year, about a month after Lucinda arrived to become a part of the crew."

"Eleven months and three days ago," she says in an unhappy monotone.

"It wasn't easy," Jeffers continues. "All the parts had to be bartered for. We couldn't put any of the requisition requests on the regular manifest for obvious reasons."

"Not so obvious to me," I say. "Explain."

He sighs. "Langlade did not support the idea of bartering medicinal products and food for what he needed. He preferred a more ... swashbuckling approach, shall we say?"

I nod, even though neither of them can see me do it. This story absolutely jives with the Langlade I know and have heard about. He would have considered it the work of an OSG's academic, not a real man. Not an independent businessman for certain.

"So our plan was to build the system, get it up and running, make a few trades to prove our concept, and then show him the hard numbers."

I realize we've left solid ground and are now walking on grates. I look past my feet and see hints of other pipes running below us.

"How big is this grid?" I ask.

"One hundred and eighty square meters, stacked," Lucinda says, again with pride tainting her words.

"How high? How many towers?"

"It's hard to give exact numbers, because we're still figuring things out, seeing what grows well and what doesn't, but our estimates say we can produce at Level G."

I stop in my tracks, my legs no longer interested in working. "Level G? That can't be right." Level K can sustain a community of two hundred souls. There's no way they have that much capacity here on this ship. They'd need something three times this size.

Lucinda turns around, her tone bitchy. "Of course it can. Do you doubt my calculations?"

Looking around, I take in the towers going to the top of the hull and their bases starting below my feet. Some quick math based on the footprint they gave me and the number of plants I see sticking out of the holes in the cylinders tells me her calculations are probably about right.

My blood starts pounding really loudly in my ears. They're growing *up* here, not simply on flats like every other ship-based system I've seen. And it's all hydroponic, using every centimeter of available space. It's been done before, of course, but not on a ship. Not on a ship of this size, anyway. Normally that kind of production is reserved for actual bioships, the BioS fleets that hover nearby the main settlements in the center of the galaxy.

"Holy shit," I say, my voice full of awe. "We're not sitting on a gold mine. We're sitting on a trillium mine."

Lucinda shrugs and then smiles for the first time since I met her. "You may not be much in the captain department, but at least you're good with numbers."

CHAPTER
SEVEN

LEAVING THE BIOGRID BEHIND IS hard, but I have business to attend to, and the rest of the universe is not going to wait on my desire to inhale the intoxicating scents of growing things. Jeffers follows as I make my way up to the flightdeck.

"So, what do you think?" he asks, out of breath from trying to keep up. Memorizing the layout of all the different drifter ships has made finding my way back to where I want to be a lot easier than I thought it would.

"I'm impressed," I say, my tone noncommittal.

"Do you know what you want to do with it?"

"With what?" I pass my hand over the keypad screen that allows admittance to the flightdeck. I frown when nothing happens.

Jeffers reaches around me, his minted breath brushing across my cheek as he punches in a code manually. I commit it to memory as the door slides open.

"With the production," he prompts. "Will you sell it? Keep it for the crew?"

"I'll let you know later. I have other things I need to take care of first." I walk up the four steps separating the main floor from the control area and sit down in the captain's chair so I can look out the clearpanels and have access to the ship's control array. A small crowd has gathered at the dock and several of its members are looking at my ship.

Jeffers stops next to me, following my gaze. "Looks like someone's not happy."

Langlade is out there, gesticulating like a mad fool in front of a man wearing an OSG uniform.

"Uh-oh." I'd hoped to be gone before he sobered up and realized what he'd done. "Trouble in Triangulum."

"You won the ship. There's nothing he can do about that now."

I look at Jeffers and half smile. "I thought you said I practically stole it."

He shrugs, looking out the window. "Gambling is bad business, that's all I meant."

"I didn't cheat. I won fair and square."

"I don't doubt you did." He looks at me and stares hard into my eyes, making me want to squirm. "You don't strike me as a cheater at anything."

Before I can comment, a crackling comes from a loudspeaker hidden somewhere on the flightdeck and then a voice rings out. One of the blackpanels near the clearpanel flickers, and the face of one of the gingers appears in it. "Hey, Captain, you up there? You around?" He looks over his shoulder and then back at the camera.

I look at the vast array of buttons on the arm of my chair, clueless about how to operate it. This doesn't look like anything I ever saw on the sim or in my training manuals.

Jeffers reaches over without a word and presses a green button with the word 'TALK' on it.

I shake my head in frustration as I speak. "I'm here. What's going on?"

"Got a little trouble down here on the dock. Feel like coming out and saying hello to the commander's henchman?" His twin is standing next to him now, looking concerned.

"Not particularly."

"Good. Let us in."

"You've made your decision?"

"Yep. We're onboard." His face gets really close to the camera, filling up the screen. "Get it? On board?" He snorts at his own joke.

"I need you to do something for me before you come back inside." I pull a piece of paper from my pocket. The list of materials needed for the biogrid that I lifted from Lucinda's desk as I walked by it comes out, and I hold it up in front of my face so the twins can see its contents. "Go to Hackmore's hardware and get me these items."

I peek from behind the list, making sure they're paying attention.

One of the gingers is squinting at the list. *Gus.* The other is looking at it normally. *Bingo. Another givit.* Gus needs MI for his eyes. I wonder why he hasn't gotten it yet.

"What's that stuff for?" the non-squinter asks.

I give him a polite, eat-my-waste smile. "Nice try, Tam, but I know Lucinda can't possibly have been running that show behind the anteroom without a major push from engineering. Get me the parts, and I'll let you back on the ship."

"I'm Gus," he says.

"Bullshit." I pull the list away from my face and shove it back in my breast pocket.

The real Gus covers the comm unit with his hand and speaks to his brother in a hushed tone. "How'd she know?"

"How the hell do I know?" Tam whispers back. He pulls his brother's hand off the system. "How are we supposed to pay for this stuff? Nothing's free at Hackmore's."

"Tell him it's for me. Tell him to use my workcredit on account there."

The two gingers look at each other and smile deviously.

"And don't even think about getting parts for the engine room without talking to me about it first. You steal from me, I remove body parts."

Their grins disappear and the screen goes pinkish black as a hand covers the entire transponder. "She's wicked smart," says one of them.

"Wicked *dirty* is more like it," says the other.

"That'll work," says the first.

The hand is gone and in its place a fuzzy smear. "Okay, Captain, we're on it."

"One other thing," I say, my pulse crazy with how well this is going. "I need you to get someone for me and bring him here."

"Who?" asks Gus, leaning toward the screen again. "Is it your boyfriend?" His body jerks to the side as he's punched by Tam, but his focus remains on my answer.

"His name is Baebong. Ask Hackmore where he is, and he'll tell you where to find him."

"He a slant-eye?" Gus asks, sounding surprised.

"You got it, Captain," says Tam, pulling his brother away from the transponder.

Gus's voice carries through the microphone as they walk away. "I'll bet it's her boyfriend. You watch. Ten credits says he's a slant-eye too."

I press the button that now says 'NO TALK' and turn the chair to face Jeffers. He's staring out the clearpanel at Langlade's group, which has grown even larger.

"Baebong?" he asks, not looking at me.

"A friend."

"What are we going to do about this?" He points to Langlade and the OSG official.

I sigh, not sure I want to incur the wrath of the OSG on my first day at the helm. Normally I'd tell those droid-heads to go suck it, but that was before I had a DS of my own. "Do you have any advice for me?"

"Talk to them. Hear what Langlade has to say. Do it from the ship with the door closed, though."

"Good plan. I like your style." I look at the buttons at my disposal and chew at my lip. *Where's the one that says 'Talk to asshole'?*

"Hit the black and blue buttons simultaneously. Dial up the dock frequency." He points out the clearpanel to the frequency numbers floating above the dockmaster's central hub, visible to every ship as it pulls in.

I do as he instructs and find myself speaking to some faceless voice working in the dockmaster's domain.

"Dock Control, Operator Five-Kilo-Five-November," the voice says.

I clear my throat before I use the standard phraseology to speak with him. "DS Anarchy here for the OSG official at Dock 5-Alpha."

"DS Anarchy?" says the voice several seconds later. "I don't have a DS Anarchy on the docket."

"Formerly known as the DS Kinsblade 3," I clarify.

"Oh. Right. Yeah, here it is. I'll give him a call for ya. You coming dockside?"

"No, I'm on the box," I say.

"Got it. Good luck. Five-Kilo-Five-November, out."

When I'm sure he's cut the connection, I breathe in really slowly, trying to get my fears to go out with the exhale. It doesn't work.

"Now we just have to hope that your claim holds," Jeffers says, staring out the clearpanel at the official talking into his wrist transponder.

I get the distinct impression that Jeffers has my back, and it makes me feel just the smallest bit braver.

CHAPTER EIGHT

A BEEP RINGS OUT ON the flightdeck and a small framed box pops up in the bottom corner of the main clearpanel. Inside the box is the face of the OSG official who's standing on the dock.

Jeffers reaches over and points to the blinking green light on my chair array that says "TALK". He nods at me, giving me the confidence I need to press it.

"Anarchy," I say, sounding as captain-like as I know how.

"Anarchy, this is Lieutenant Brak on the dock, just in front of you."

"I see you there, Sir. Hello."

"I've got Langlade of the Kinsblade Fleet down here claiming you're onboard his ship without permission."

My heart is hammering painfully in my chest and my ears are on fire. *What do I say? Play stupid? Call him a liar liar pants on fire? Start shooting?* I'm too freaked out to think straight and my mouth takes over. "I'm sorry to inform you, Sir, that you've got a damn liar on your hands."

Surprisingly, he actually smirks and looks over his shoulder before turning back to face my ship. "Can you come out to discuss?"

"Not at this time. We have a bit of a containment breach up here, and I'd like to get it under control first."

"Understood. Need any help with that?"

"No, we're good."

"I assume you have the documentation for the ship?"

I nod. *Please let that damn paper be real.* "I'll send it to your unit. What's the transmit code?"

Jeffers presses a button on the array for me bringing up a floating virtual keyboard, and I ready myself to enter the data.

"Alpha, charlie, lima, five, five, niner, bravo." He pauses. "Need me to repeat?"

"No, I've got it." I pull the document I took from the givit table just two hours ago and hold it up in front of the keyboard, pressing the button that I know will capture the image of it. Once I see it floating in front of me in holographic form, I hit the *Transmit* key.

"Transmitting now," I say, folding the paper and putting it back in my pocket.

Jeffers nods, and I get the feeling he's impressed with my knowledge of the onboard holo-comm system. Now if I could just figure out the damn buttons, maybe I'd feel like I deserved that respect. The manuals I used always showed them in a different configuration.

"Just give me a minute to verify that signature," the lieutenant says. The little box with his face in it turns to fuzz, telling me he's still connected but talking to someone else I'm not hooked in with.

I grip my hands together to keep them from shaking. Cold sweats take over as I wait for his official decision. The evidence might not hold up in front of a full-fledged tribunal —I'm not sure what the OSG's position on givit pots would be— but it'll give me time to get the hell out of here and out into the Dark before Langlade can stop me. A tribunal would take months to convene, and that's assuming he's stupid enough to want to call for one. My instincts tell me he stays far away from the judicial arm of the OSG like most of the people I have contact with out here in the Badlands. The Havenots rarely fare well in front of an OSG tribunal.

Lieutenant Brak's face comes back up on the screen and he's almost smiling. "Got the all-clear from Dock Control. Sorry for the trouble, Captain."

"No problem, Sir. I appreciate your help."

"You got it." He's about to cut the line, but then he stops. "Hey."

My finger hovers over the NO-TALK button. "Yes, Sir?"

"Did I hear right? You won this ship in a game of givit?"

"Partially right, Sir." I say, nerves making me sound like a new recruit — serious and scared. "I won it in a *hand* of givit, not a whole game."

He shakes his head, smiling. "Cass Kennedy. Card shark. Remind me never to engage you in a hand of givit."

I have no idea how to respond to this guy. The OSG has always been the one thing standing between me and the life I've wanted to live, that I was born to live. This guy acting like we could be friends is throwing me off my game completely.

"I'll do that, Sir."

His expression goes dark as something catches his attention off to the side. "Brak out." His connection cuts off, and his face disappears. I watch through the clearpanel as a fight breaks out between Langlade and the group of people around him, some of whom I recognize from my nights in the underground clubs — troublemakers just following the action because there's nothing else better to do.

The official jumps into the melee, his shock wand out and doing some serious damage. *Damn, he's good with that thing.* Good meaning vicious, that is. Soon, several human forms are writhing on the ground in pain.

I've felt the sensation of thirty jotts of laserbolt energy running through my body on more than a few occasions, so I pity those idiots who thought fighting in the presence of an OSG official would be a good idea.

I allow myself to relax just a tiny bit, now that I'm back to the business of running my ship and preparing for launch without the threat of being taken down by the OSG. "Well, that went okay. I guess." I let out the breath I feel like I've been holding the entire time.

"I suggest we leave as soon as possible," Jeffers says, moving away from my chair.

"Where are you going?" I ask, watching him walk to the door on the right side of the flightdeck.

"To prepare our next meal."

I check my watch. "It's zero two hundred."

"And by the time you get everyone back onboard and things underway, it'll be time for breakfast."

Four hours from now. Holy shit. The immensity of what I've undertaken kind of hits me all at once. Not only do I have to do the not-at-all minor task of getting this ship off the dock and out into the Dark without killing anyone or running up a repair bill in the process, but

I also have to figure out how this particular DS works and what shape its various systems are in. Now that I've had the tour, I know at the very least that I need to get it cleaned up so it functions properly. And then ... gee, I don't know. I guess after all that's done, I'll figure out where to go from there.

Why had my plans and dreams never gotten me past the acquisition of the ship? Did I really not believe I could pull it off, deep down inside? Now that's a depressing thought.

The crackling of the speaker pulls me out of my melancholy thought stream and brings me back to the more demanding present.

"Yo, Captain Kick Ass, you up there?" It's Gus and he's smiling.

"Back so soon?" I'm pretending I'm not happy to see him. He can't possibly have been to Hackmore's and back so quickly, but it sure is nice to see a somewhat familiar and friendly face after my OSG run-in.

He turns partway to let someone else's face show up on my panel. "Found your friend loitering on the docks not far from here. Mission accomplished." He bows.

"I wasn't loitering," my best friend Baebong says, a hint of a scowl changing his normally placid expression. "I was coming to the Anarchy."

"Anarchy?" Gus perks up. "What's that? Is that a bar? Are there dancing girls there? With clothes or without?"

Baebong shoves Gus out of the frame. "Shut up, droid." He addresses me directly. "Knock, knock." His grin flashes and then disappears, leaving his face expressionless again. I hate playing givit with him; he has zero tell. "Open the hell up."

"You got your stuff with you?" My hand rests just above the OPEN button.

He jerks his head toward something behind him. "Yeah. And a few little things I scored when you were busy being a crazy-ass bitch."

"Hey, watch it. This crazy-ass bitch won herself a DS, and she's not letting you on it if you don't show a little respect." I'm grinning hard now. This is going to work. Baebong is here. I knew he'd come.

Baebong salutes. "Yes, ma'am. R-E-S-P-E-C-T. Find out what it means to me. Permission to come aboard."

I try to see around him, wondering if the others are there just outside the range of the transponder. "Where are Nance and Zeke?"

Baebong's face remains impassive. "Being limprods."

My heart sinks a little. I thought more of my friends would follow me. Whenever I shared my vision they seemed to agree it was the best way to live.

"Permission to come aboard granted," I say, pressing the button. Some of my spark has left, though. Running a DS with a skeleton crew doesn't feel like a really great idea. I keep thinking back to my tour guide's comment about a non-spark issue. *Please, Universe, don't let me turn into a jellyfish.*

I've never seen one of those poor suckers who's been lost in the Dark without a ship's gravity field in person, but I've heard stories and seen images. Doomed to spend their last months of life without gravity because their bones have become too weak to handle it, their skeletons begin to disintegrate and break apart, eventually resulting in these poor people dying in horrible pain as their bodies can no longer physically support their internal systems. Cells perish, immunity disappears, and the body goes into full pain response. Most choose the floating death over the suffering.

The great rumbling starts again, and Baebong looks to his left. He speaks to someone I can't see, I assume Gus. "Grab that side and push." He points to a cart of Baebong's equipment on wheels.

"What is all this junk, anyway?" Gus asks.

Baebong leans over, and I hear a smack of skin against skin.

"Ow! What was that for?" cries Gus, the recipient of Baebong's abuse.

"That's for touching shit that doesn't concern you. Just push it up the ramp and into my space."

Been there, done that. I have to admit— it really is hard to not touch Baebong's stuff. It's all so interesting and sometimes as outright cool as Haloid's ice.

"Dude, you just got here. You don't have a space yet."

Baebong looks at me with his eyes slightly more open, which is saying a lot since he is a slant-eye as Gus suspected earlier. "I better have a space."

"Yeah, yeah, you have a space. Just get your ass on here, would you? I miss your ugly face."

"Back at ya." He winks at the screen as it fades to black.

I have no idea where I'm going to put him, but he's right; he needs a space big enough to sleep and work in, since he tends to wake up in the middle of sleeptime to tinker with things, and I hate when he disturbs my rest.

I leave the flightdeck to welcome him onboard the DS Anarchy and to locate the perfect spot for a guy who designs weapons and ammunition for a living.

CHAPTER NINE

SO, THIS IS IT, HUH?" Baebong stands in the center of the cargo hold as the airlock door is closing behind him. Gus disappears from view as he leaves to help his brother.

"Yep, this is her. The DS Anarchy with me at the helm." I can't stop smiling. This is really happening. *Hell yeah, it is!*

"I hope we don't die," he says casually, his eyes going over the details around him.

"Me too. Come on." I walk toward one of the several corridors that branch off this central area. "Let's go find you a bunk."

"I thought you already had one ready for me."

"How in the hell would that be possible? I just got here. Besides, I figured you'd want to choose your own." I glance over my shoulder in time to catch him looking intrigued.

"Good idea." He follows behind me at a jog to catch up. "I need a spot that's big enough…"

"To sleep and work in. I know." I shake my head. "We've been friends for three years, and you think I haven't noticed how you operate?"

"Ha. No. I know exactly how much you notice. Exactly everything."

I'm smiling at what feels like a compliment until he finishes his thought.

"It's like living with the OSG sometimes for shit's sake."

I whip around to face him, my legs spread apart and my hand at my thigh. He knows better than to call me OSG. "Watch your mouth, asshole."

He holds up a hand near his chest, palm out. "Relax. Not meant as an insult. Hey, look." He points over my shoulder. "A bunk. Could it be mine, do you think?"

"Don't try to distract me," I say, not falling for his game of squirrel.

He sighs, his shoulders dropping. "Listen, Cass, you need to relax if this is going to work."

"If *what's* going to work?"

"This." He throws his arms out to his sides and looks all around. "Being the captain of your ship. Being a drifter. Managing a crew of ten people."

"Six."

His expression goes confused. "Six? Six what?"

"Six people, including me."

His jaw drops open for a few seconds. Then he goes into overdrive, his hands flying up to rest on his head. "You can't pilot a DS with only *six* people! That's in*sane*!"

I fold my arms across my chest and lift my chin. "Langlade did it."

"Langlade's an idiot." His hands come down hard and slap his thighs. "He lost his ship to a girl in a hand of cards, for fuck's sake."

"Thanks." I glare at my best friend, wondering what the hell happened to make him so grouchy.

He lets out a big breath, pushing his hands together in front of him like he's saying a prayer and doing a pec workout at the same time. Then he reaches out and taps my shoulder with those compressed hands. "Come *on*, you know what I mean. We need to be smart about this."

"You calling me stupid?" I wait for him to say something even more risky. He might be my friend, but that doesn't mean I won't cut his ass.

"No." He steps closer, his hands dropping away as he looks down at me, eye to eye. "I'm calling you the bravest, toughest, craziest bitch in this entire galaxy. A person I want to see succeed. Don't stack the deck against yourself by going out under-crewed."

I pull out of his personal space, refusing to be coddled into agreeing. "I've had the deck stacked against me since I was born. Why change things now when everything's going so well?"

He shakes his head, but a small smile appears, too. "You know … I should just walk right off this ship and not even look back."

"Yeah, right." I snort. "Like you'd turn your back on the chance to be drifting and blowing up space junk with your stupid guns all day."

"Hey, watch it. My guns aren't stupid."

"Whatever." I wave my hand over the panel at the door to open it. Thankfully it cooperates, unlike many of the other ones around here. I hope this means Gus or Tam has been busy rekeying the codes for everything so they will function with the new crew. "Do you want this bunk or not?"

The door slides open and a terrifically awful stench comes out and hits us right in the face. We both put our hands up to our noses to stop as much of it as we can from entering our brains. I don't have enough medcredits to rid our bodies of bad C-Cells right now.

"What in the hell died in there?" he asks, breathing through his mouth.

"This was the pilot's bunk, I think." I'd recognize that particular brand of stink anywhere. "We can get it cleaned out if you think it's big enough." I look to the left and right, taking in the large space, half of which houses a bed and side table and the other half of which hosts workbenches covered in crap. I see nothing usable there, but Baebong will. One man's trash is always his treasure.

He looks down the corridor to his left and right and then back at me. "It's close to the cargo bay and not far from the engine room. I like that. Probably big enough, too."

"The gingers are in that engine room, fair warning. And I don't know if they have separate bunks somewhere else or if their living space is connected to it."

"Gingers? As in *plural*? More than one? You can't be serious."

I nod, sharing his disbelief. If I hadn't seen it myself, I wouldn't have trusted it either. "Natural twin gingers."

"I thought they'd faded from the gene pool."

I shrug. "Apparently not."

"Ahh, I get it. Clones."

"I don't think so. They don't have the mark. At least one of them doesn't." I realize then that I was only offered a look at Gus's neck. It's possible one escaped marking, but I highly doubt it. Even so, I make a mental note to check them both out when they get back. Registering stupid clone butt everywhere we dock could be a pain. I'm not totally against it, but they'd have to have some serious skills I couldn't live without to be worth the trouble.

Baebong looks around some more and then nods. "This'll do if you can get rid of whatever rotten meat is stored inside it."

"It's not meat, it's the guy who was living in there. Seriously, he stunk."

"Whatever. Vacuum filter it and get one of those gingers to clean it up and I'm in."

I laugh.

"What's so funny?"

"What's so funny is you thinking someone else is going to clean up your room for you." I reach beyond the door to the supply closet I know to be right inside. There's a suction hose connected to the main system, wrapped up on a hook. "Here you go," I say, handing him the nozzle. "Have fun." Walking away, I giggle silently at the expression on his face.

"I thought I was going to be the Lieutenant of this bucket of bolts!"

"You are! Happy sucking, Lieutenant So-Sun!"

His cranky, mumbled response follows me down the corridor. "I've got something for you to suck."

I hold my laughter in until I get to the flightdeck, and then I can't do it anymore. I collapse into my chair with a huge smile on my face and spin it around and around as I stare at all the blinking lights going blurry.

I've made it. I've finally made it.

My chair slows to a halt. *And now it's time for me to get my butt out into the Dark and start living the life I've always dreamed was waiting for me.* I wait for my brain to stop spinning and then I just sit there, wondering what my next step should be. When I catch a whiff of my own stink, I realize what it is.

Dialing up Hackmore's frequency, I do a quick mental calculation of the credits I have left over there. I need a shower bad, so that water filtration system needs to be in top working condition.

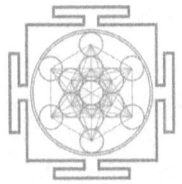

CHAPTER
TEN

THE GINGERS ARE HAPPILY ENSCONCED in the engine room with their new toys, after a quick transmission over to Hackmore allowed them some credits to play with for parts and supplies on their lists. I assume Lucinda is in her biogrid chamber, trying to figure out how she's going to keep hating my guts when three big boxes of supplies just showed up at her door. Baebong is to my right, sitting at the navigator's station, and Jeffers is standing to my left, pointing out things on my captain's seat array. Essentially, I'm getting a crash course on how not to crash.

"Everything's pretty much labeled. The tags will change as you need them to." He points. "See? *OPEN* when the door is closed changes to *CLOSE* when the door is open."

"Redundancies?"

Jeffers points to the system monitoring station to my left, which I could reach in three running steps. "There. Set up the same way. You can switch back and forth here." He points to the control switch. "I'll man that station as needed until you either replace me or feel comfortable running them both yourself." He shrugs. "In a perfect world, we have somebody there full-time, but you can only do what you can do."

"Yeah, right. Okay." I study the myriad buttons, trying to place them against the pictures I have in my mind — the diagrams I memorized of the systems present in every *DS* configuration ever designed. "Why does this look so different?" I ask half to myself.

"Gus mostly. He likes updating things."

"Even things that don't need to be updated?" I look up to see if Jeffers agrees.

He's having a hard time not smiling. "There's always room for improvement, says the mind of the engineer."

"That's great," I say, wanting to punch the damn thing, "only I didn't learn on this custom-Gus system. I learned the old-school systems."

"It's all there, just more intuitive." He points. "You start the launch sequence here, then as you move through the stages of navigating off the dock and then steerage, your hand moves forward across the array instead of jumping around." He mimics pushing buttons without actually doing it. "See? It's designed for a skilled operator onboard. The older systems were designed with the buttons you needed around the same time spread across opposite ends of the array so that you wouldn't press any two together or too quickly in sequence."

"But that just slows down reaction time." I never noticed that about the systems I learned before, but he's right about how it makes your hand jump around.

"Yes, with someone skilled. But with someone not so competent, it keeps mistakes from happening that could damage the electronics. Our last pilot was quite well-qualified for the chair, so Gus made the changes."

I nod, kind of seeing the method behind the madness. "I guess." I'm not so sure we shouldn't go back to the old array until I have more practice, though. I memorized a whole different arrangement in my sim training. Now I have to learn something completely new in real time on my first attempt at off-docking. *Please don't let me destroy my ship.*

"Give it a try," Jeffers says cheerfully. "What's the worst that could happen?" He smiles at me encouragingly.

"Uhhh… I could smash the Anarchy into another ship, breaking its gyro system, sending it spinning into all the other ships and destroy this entire station?"

His smile slips. "What's the *second* worst thing that could happen?"

"Do you really want me to answer that?" I cringe, wondering if me launching and piloting this ship is such a good idea. Maybe I should watch someone else do it first. *Could I stand the smell of my tour guide for a single tour around the Dark?*

"Better not." He gestures to the array. "Just do it. The worst isn't going to happen."

"You're a seer too, huh?" I look out the clearpanel, dreading the difficult journey I have before me. Sad that it's less than a hundred meters far.

"No, not at all. I prefer being deaf, dumb, and blind to the future."

"Come on, let's go," my lieutenant Baebong says. He points to the clearpanel. "Isn't that Langlade's man?"

I see my former tour guide striding up the dock pedestrian tunnel toward the ship. Mister Stink looks like he's on a mission.

"That's the guy who used to sleep in your bunk," I say to Baebong with no small measure of satisfaction. I can practically see his bad odor from here. He's fogging up the tunnels with it.

"Eck. He's probably coming to get his dead chicken back."

"Dead chicken?"

Jeffers and I check to see if Baebong's kidding, but he's shaking his head with his hand up. "Swear to the gods of the universe. Fucking dead chicken in a box under the bed."

Jeffers hisses, shifting his gaze to the floor.

"What's up with the dead chicken?" I ask.

"Probably traded it for something." Jeffers sits in the system monitor's chair to my left. "Thank you for kicking him out before he asked me to cook it. Who knows where it was from or how old it was."

"It was old enough to stink, I know that. I sent it through the incinerator," Baebong says. "Come on, let's go." He punches a few buttons on his array, and all the panels at eye-level go clear. We have about thirty degrees of realtime visibility and another three hundred of virtual visibility thanks to the magecomms situated on the opposite side of the ship. The only spots we can't see are right behind each thruster. It's enough to nearly send me into a blind panic. I've got other ships on all sides of me and precious little room to maneuver out of here. Just one bump into a pedestrian tunnel, and I could cause hundreds of painful deaths before pressure and oxygen flow are re-established.

"You can do this," Baebong says. "Just take it slow. I'll be your eyes."

"I think I'd better use my own eyes." I punch the button that will start our off-docking launch sequence.

The ship detaches with a hiss and some mechanical clanking from the dock's entry bridge, breaking the seal between us, making it impossible for anyone there to come onboard without a really great jump, a darksuit, and some serious ability to hang. And if they're still clinging to the side of my ship when I go into the air-lock bay, a bio-alert will go off. I'm not worried. Not at all.

Okay, maybe a little.

A ginger's voice comes over the speaker. "Hello, up there on Mount Olympus. It's the brains down here in the engine room."

Gus, I suspect.

"You ready to rumble?" he asks.

"Ready," I say, my eyes glued to the clearpanels in front of me.

"Check we're clear," he says, by way of instruction.

I make sure there are no alerts about people too close to the docking mechanism. I don't know where the rotten chicken man is, but he must not be there.

"All clear." I press the last button in the sequence that will finish our off-docking maneuver. A hint of ice-crystal fog floats into view on one of the virtual clearpanels, as the release valves for Anarchy's ramp securing itself into the bottom of the ship hiss out the water pressure. The ice-crystals float away, being gently sucked into the station's freewaste containment system.

"You've got power," he says. "Call me if you need anything. I'll be busy being awesome down here."

"Out," I say, cutting the transmission.

"Which one was that?" Baebong asks.

"Gus," I say, before Jeffers can respond.

"How can you tell?" Baebong asks, like he doesn't believe my answer. "I saw them both and talked to them, and they're exactly alike."

"Most people can't tell them apart," Jeffers says.

"They're totally different," I mutter, my concentration stuck on my next move. I prefer to back away, spin ninety degrees, and head out straight, but I know a more experienced pilot would just do it without the spin, leading by the ship's portside. My spin will advertise me as a gloob, but I can't let my pride hurt my ship. Next time I pull in here, I'll be kicking ass all over the galaxy and taking names. They'll forget I left with a ninety this one time.

A green light glows near one of the clearpanels and the frequency for the dockmaster floats just above it.

I press the TALK button at my left hand. "Anarchy, Captain Cass." I like to keep my last name out of things if at all possible. No need to alert the entire universe to who I am when it's totally irrelevant.

"Anarchy, this is the dockmaster. We have your former pilot here asking for permission to contact."

I roll my eyes. *Just when I thought things were going well.* "Put him through."

Baebong snorts. "Told you he wants his chicken back."

"Hey, girly!" comes the voice over the speaker.

My blood starts to boil before the echo of his words has stopped ringing across the flightdeck.

"What do you want, Pilot?" I grind out.

"I need to get in my bunk. Get some of my things."

"Too late. I told you when I was leaving."

"Hey! That ain't right! I told you I had a meeting!"

"With a whore. I know. Poor girl. I'll put your shit in a box and shoot it out for you." There's a delivery chute for just such things in the exit bays of the station. I remember seeing it when I was on the smaller transport craft that I hopped to get here.

"No! Don't do that. Just dock up and let me on."

"Sorry, no can do." I cut the connection and move the joystick that will give us the tiniest bit of juice from the ship's forward particle thruster. The landscape on the clearpanels begins to change perspective as we move away from our dock space.

"Easy does it," says Baebong. "You got this."

"Yeah, I know," I say distractedly. The second joystick in my other hand comes into play as I slowly rotate the ship around on its vertical axis. The stacked openings to the station come into view along with the suns, stars, and planetary systems that make up the Triangulum Galaxy. *Easy, easy, easy, easy. You can do this. You will not destroy an entire space station with one false move.*

I press the transmit button that will connect me with the dockmaster's hub.

"Dockmaster. Go ahead, Anarchy."

"Thank you, Dockmaster. Anarchy requesting exit bay."

"Anarchy, Looks like Bay K, that's Bay Kilo is open for you."

"Awesome," Baebong says quietly. "That's big enough for a CS."

I'm left to wonder if the dockmaster gave me a bay twice the size of my ship on purpose. *Is my gloob status that obvious?*

"Thank you, Sir. Have a good one."

"Same to you, Anarchy. We're all rootin' for ya."

Baebong snorts.

Dammit. Gloob status acknowledged. "Thanks." I cut the comm and focus on my thrusters. "Going up thirty-two meters."

"All clear above," Baebong says, checking the monitors for someone who might be above us and in the way of clear sailing.

When we're level with the exit bay, I shift the aft thruster's power to conduct forward motion. Using only two-percent strength, we glide through the space inside the station into the gaping entrance of the launch bay. Once there, the initial door closes behind us. The Anarchy hovers with a quick jink of the forward thrusters to keep us at equilibrium. Now is not the time to bang into the sides of the bay when so far I've done pretty damn good, if I do say so myself.

"You got a box of the old pilot's stuff to put in the chute?" I ask Baebong.

"Not unless you count that chicken. There were no clothes, no shoes, no nothing in there. The engine parts I assumed belong to the Anarchy, so I kept 'em."

"I'm pretty sure he wore the same thing every day," I say remembering the smell. "And those parts are ours, you're right."

"You are correct about his wardrobe," Jeffers says. "And good riddance to that."

"If the pilot needs to reach us, he can leave us a message at the station. We'll catch it next time we're here," I say, leaving the last part of my thought out: *assuming we ever come back.*

The green lights on either side of the secondary doors go on just before the big exit bay begins to open to the Dark waiting just beyond it. My blood pressure spikes, making me feel like there's a body of water rushing through my head. I can hear the waves crashing over and over.

"Aft thruster, five percent," I say, easing the joystick toward the open space before us for three seconds before letting up on it. The Dark is ready to swallow us whole, it seems. Never before have I been so nervous leaving a station behind. Normally, I can't wait to be rid of their restrictions and control.

"Watch it!" Baebong yells out, pointing to a small craft zipping in front of us.

Impact alarms start squealing, giving me the heart attack they seem designed to encourage. I quickly tweak the joystick back, throwing some fore thrust into the mix to slow us down.

"Who's that bozo?" Jeffers asks.

"I don't know," I say, easing the aft thruster back into play, "but he'd better get the hell out of my way."

"Are you sure…?" Jeffers doesn't have time to finish his thought before I'm right in the flight path of the little zipper. We miss him by less than the length of his stupid craft.

Dumbass. What would have been a mere scratch to the *Anarchy* would have spelled the end of him.

"That was close," Baebong says. "Too close."

The criticism in his tone is clear, but I'm not taking it personally. "So? Go change your underwear and come back. We'll wait."

"Ha-ha, very fucking funny."

I try to keep a straight face, but it's impossible in the presence of his outrage. A grin sneaks out for a second or two before I can smother it.

"Did I mention I've come up with a new stun system?" he asks. "Yeah. Straps to the wrist. Go to shake someone's hand and drop 'em like a rock in super-gravity."

"Sounds fun. Touch me with it, though, and you die." All of my attention is on getting away from the station without a scratch, so I can't spare him a glance, but I know he's considering whether to try it out on me or not. "I'm serious."

"There's that PC again," Jeffers says, pointing out the starboard side clearpanels.

I shake my head at this idiot pilot's persistence. Even a kid knows better than to move a personal craft into the path of a drifter ship. "He's going to become a small pile of space junk if he's not careful."

"I think that's…" Baebong touches some buttons on his array, and a voice crackles over the speaker, cutting in and out.

"Kinsblade … pilot … dammit to hell…"

"It's that guy again," I say when I recognize the voice. "Langlade's pilot. What in the hell is his problem?"

"He must have something pretty valuable in that bunk of his," Jeffers says. "Maybe you missed something, Baebong."

I press the controls that will isolate the comm signal broadcasting from his craft. Two seconds later his voice comes in loud and clear.

"You little bitch better open up that airlock and let me in there, or so help me…"

I sigh and look over at Baebong. "You ready to do some night crawling, my friend?"

"Hell yeah, I am." He touches a few buttons and then turns around to watch me.

I tap into the engine room with the comm system. "Time to play night crawler, boys." Hitting the all-ship

comm button, I make the mandatory safety and prepa-
ratory announcement. "All hands, we are night crawling.
I repeat, we are night crawling in ten. Going to Xylera.
Better buckle up." A flick of my finger turns the all-ship
comm off and the engine room comm on over a single
frequency.

"Fucking A!" a ginger yells. "Just let me check one
thing…"

"We good for Xylera?" I ask, assuming because
Langlade was docked for supplies that the Anarchy's set
for travel.

"Yep, all levels topped off." Tam says. "Well, mostly.
Could use some more water."

"Water, got it. We'll hit the ice fields on the far side.
Make sure we don't drag anything in with us." *Ten … nine
…. eight…*

"Isolating now. You see that PC starboard, right?"

I know I'm talking to Tam, but I'm not sure how I know.

"Yes, Tam, thanks." *Seven…*

"This is Gus."

"Don't lie. I'm not in the mood." *Six…*

"Dude, how does she know?" comes another voice at
a whisper.

"Shut up," Tam whispers back before putting his normal voice back online. "Okay, milady. Whenever you're
ready, we are."

"Captain will do," I say, shaking my head. I feel like
I'm trapped on a ship full of brain damaged renaissance
actors.

"All the captains I've ever worked for had hairy chests,"
Gus says. "Sorry, but I just don't see it."

"Tam?"

"Yes, Captain?"

"Are we ready?"

"Yes, we are. Let 'er rip."

"Going in *five*." I press several buttons, responding lightening quick to the prompts I'm given by the computer. I've done this a thousand times in the simulator and another ten thousand in my head. *I'm ready. I can do this. Breathe, Cass, don't forget to breathe.*

"*Four.*"

More buttons. More questions from the computer. More panic.

"*Three.*"

Sweat droplets pop out on my forehead, upper lip, back, neck, chest…

"*Two…*"

I think I'm about to have a heart attack. I hope Jeffers can get my friends back where they belong when I'm dead.

"*One*, we are nightcrawling, people." My hands are shaking from nerves and excitement. I've been a passenger for this but never the one calling the shots. Not even close. I really hope we don't die.

There's a muffled boom, then a *whoosh*, and finally silence as all sound is stolen from our eardrums. The pricks of light that indicate the stars and planets become white lines, bending down toward the center of a hole we created — the wormhole we're using to pass through space-time, skipping over millions of Earth lightyears in mere minutes and seconds. Something pulls at my center, filling me and sucking everything out at the same time.

And then… everything goes black.

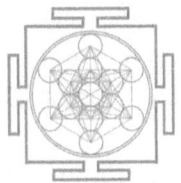

CHAPTER
ELEVEN

WHEN WE COME OUT OF the wormhole, I'm nauseated, but that's nothing new. At least my face isn't green like Baebong's. I put the ship on one percent aft thrust to allow for a short drift-recovery for the crew as the wormhole closes behind us.

"Oh, shit, I'll never get used to that," Baebong moans, leaning back in his chair, letting his head hang over the top of it.

Jeffers rests his head in his arms on the console in front of him. I leave him to his recovery because I know going through a wormhole means different things to different people. As I wait for my nausea to pass, I look through the clearpanels at the Dark around us and the planet that will give us water. The surface of Xylera is still thousands of kilometers away, but its white and blue, ice-laden surface is clearly visible even from this distance.

I activate the all-ship comm. "Everyone okay?" As I wait for the crew's responses, I brush the sweaty hair off my forehead. It's been way too long since I've had a shower. That water collection feels even more important now.

"We're all good down here," Gus says. "Well, I am, anyway." He giggles.

"Screw you, asshole." Tam sounds as sick as Baebong looks. I guess we have two lilies on the ship.

"All good in the biogrid," comes the next call-in. I expect to hear more, but that's all Lucinda has to say. I guess she's a woman of few words.

I am about to say something to Baebong, but I'm interrupted by another transmission over the speakers.

"S'pose now's as good a time as any to say hello." This announcement is followed by a burp and a, "Whoops. 'Scuse."

Jeffers lifts his head and looks at me, confusion marring his features. I raise my eyebrow, silently asking him who the hell is talking to us now.

Jeffers shrugs. "I don't recognize the voice."

"Last transmission, who are you?" I demand.

"The name's Rollo. Nice to meet you, Captain."

Holy crap, I can't believe it. My first flight, and I already have a stowaway? What the hell. I press the comm unit. "Get your ass up to the flightdeck, pronto."

"Yes, Ma'am."

Baebong turns around and looks at me, his complexion finally back to normal. "Did you know there was somebody else here?"

"Of course I didn't know. Do you honestly believe I would just look the other way with a stowaway onboard?"

"No. I meant, did you invite this Rollo guy to be a crew member?"

Baebong is making no sense.

"Don't you think that's something I would've mentioned? I don't even know somebody named Rollo. Do you?"

He shrugs mysteriously. "I might."

I'm surprised by his answer. I thought I knew everyone he knew. "Maybe *you* invited him on here." It's been known to happen before. An offhand comment in a bar can sound like an invitation to a lot of people. I'm not ashamed to say that I myself might have read too much into people's words a few times in the past just trying to survive.

"Like hell I did." Baebong frowns at me.

Jeffers speaks up. "Why am I getting a bad feeling about this Rollo guy?"

Baebong spins around in his chair, his back to me now. "You'll see."

"Should I be worried about this guy carrying a weapon?" I ask, getting to my feet.

"Nah. He's harmless. Mostly."

I shut the all-comm down and wait for the arrival of our uninvited guest. I have to figure out what the hell I'm going to do with this guy. I'm sure there's some sort of holding cell somewhere on the ship, but I have no idea where it is or even how to access it. I'm going to have to get either Gus or Tam involved, which means our water collection is going to be delayed. *Perfect. So much for my shower.*

The door leading to the flightdeck opens, and our stowaway steps through. I scan his entire body quickly to see if I recognize him. He's dressed like a drifter. Dirty blond hair, dark skin, scar through his right eyebrow, wiry but muscled — looks like trouble. I spent quite a bit of time at that last station, but I don't recognize this guy at all, and he has a face I would never forget.

He strides toward my chair with his hand out and a grin lighting up his face. "Nice to meet you, Captain." He stops a few feet away, but his expression goes unsure as he realizes I am not here as his welcoming committee.

"What are you doing on my ship?" I leave my arms at my sides, ready for any sudden moves on his part. I don't trust him for obvious reasons.

He shrugs. "Heard you were going to do some drifting. With all the changes coming down the pike, thought you might need a business manager onboard."

Changes? What changes? I don't want to sound stupid, so I don't ask. Instead, I address the more obvious problem. "And you decided it would be a good idea to just show up uninvited and assign yourself that duty?" I shake my head slowly. "You must have a righteous set of balls to think that would fly."

"More like a death wish," Baebong mumbles, still not looking at me.

Rollo remains completely undeterred from his mission. "If you're going to survive out here, you're going to need to do some deals, and Rollo's the guy for that. Nobody gets a better shake than Rollo, that's a fact."

I look over at Baebong. "Does he always speak in the third person like that?"

"Unfortunately."

"Where's the holding cell on the ship?" I ask anyone who might know the answer.

"I'll show you," says Jeffers, standing.

"Holding cell?" Rollo looks from me to Jeffers and then back at me again. "You don't need to put Rollo in the holding cell. Rollo can just sit up here with you guys."

"Like hell Rollo will." I shift my gaze to Jeffers. "Lock him up for me, would you, please?"

"As you wish." Jeffers stands gesturing with his arm toward the door. "After you, Sir."

"Are you sure you don't want to reconsider?" Rollo graces me with a big smile. "Rollo's real good with navigation too. Looks like you're a little shorthanded up here on the flightdeck." He tilts his head toward the station where Jeffers was recovering.

"I'm sure." I turn to face out the front clearpanels again. I don't have time for this garbage right now.

"All right. Well, Rollo will be in the cell then," he says. "Waiting. Feel free to invite him to breakfast."

I refuse to acknowledge him. The door behind me slides open, but Rollo keeps talking. "Rollo hasn't eaten in a while, in case it matters to anyone." His voice is cut off as the door slides home.

"How do you know him?" I ask Baebong, his back to me now.

"I don't *know* him, know him, I just know *of* him."

"How?"

"Are we going to have breakfast soon? I'm starving."

My voice goes firmer. "How do you know *of* him?"

Baebong sighs and slowly turns his chair to face mine. "I might have done a deal with him back on the station."

"What deal?"

"Some hardware is all. No big deal."

"Why is my ass twitching?"

He looks confused for a second before he answers. "Because you haven't had a shower in a week?"

"No. Because you're not telling me the truth. Lies make my ass twitch."

"Wow. That's unfortunate."

"For you. Start talking or you're going into the cell with him."

His face falls. "You can't be serious."

"Try me."

"Fine. You want the whole story? I'll tell it to you, not that it matters, because I didn't invite his stupid ass on here."

"I'm listening."

"I needed a beam interruptor for my latest project, and he knew how to get me one. He heard me talking in a bar one night and inserted himself into the conversation and then said he could help me out. And he did. End of story."

"End of prelude to story," I say, staring him down.

"Okay, so things might have gotten a little hairy when the previous owner of said part found out he was being relieved of it, but I took care of it."

"How?"

"By paying for it, obviously."

"With?" I know good and well that Baebong's as broke as I am.

He spins around in his chair to look out the clearpanels as he mumbles his answer.

"What's that?" I ask. "Didn't quite catch it. Did you say blow job?"

"No!" He's facing me again. "Are you insane?"

I laugh. The expression on his face is so offended, and it's hard to get Baebong to have any expression at all; he usually looks so outwardly unaffected by everything.

"I said I paid him with an IOU."

My eyes roll into my head. "Great. Well done. Another IOU."

"It's not your problem," he grumbles, staring down at his lap.

"Maybe not yesterday, but today it is. You have those parts on my ship and you're my lieutenant. What am I supposed to do if that guy comes after you?"

"He's not going to come after me. It's not that big a deal."

"I'm not paying your debt."

"And I don't expect you to."

"See that you ship his credits out as soon as possible."

"I planned on it."

We stare at each other for a few long seconds. I hate the fact that I feel like his mother. *Captains are not supposed to nag, right?* I'm pretty sure the answer is no, but I also know most captains would be harsher than I am, so maybe a little nagging isn't such a bad thing.

"So what's the deal with this guy Rollo? Can I trust him?"

Baebong shrugs. "He got me my part, and I looked all over the galaxy and back for that thing without any luck."

"You said he stole it, though. That's not cool."

"I think steal is a strong word. It's more like he borrowed it with the intention of never returning it to a guy who wasn't using it and would never have missed it."

I sigh. "You do hear yourself, right?"

"Whatever." He turns back around and presses some buttons that I know put his system on stand-by. "I need to eat. I'm starving, and if I have to go back into my bunk with that smell in there, I'm going to need something in my stomach. And I'm talking real food, not pellets."

My stomach goes into a knot at the idea of eating more pellets. Sure, they cut down on waste and supposedly meet all of a human's nutritional requirements, but they taste like dust. Pellets are the food of the poor, and I've had enough of them to last me an entire lifetime.

"Have one of the gingers run a vacuum filter cycle in your bunk. Three hours and it should be good, assuming there aren't any more chickens hiding in there."

"Will do." Baebong gets up from his chair and walks to the door.

"We good?" I ask him as he opens it up.

"Always," he says just before he disappears down the corridor.

I stare out the clearpanels and sigh, letting my body go boneless in the chair. My first launch, my first nightcrawl, and now my first stowaway, and I haven't even been captain a full twenty-four hours yet. It makes me wonder what other unexpected surprises the future has in store for me.

CHAPTER
TWELVE

THE MEAL IS SURPRISINGLY GOOD. Eggs? I haven't had any of those in months. Could be more than a year. It's surprising how quickly I've forgotten my past life. It seems like I've always lived like a starving beggar, surviving on dusty pellets, when really it's only been three years. Before that, eggs were a given in my father's household.

"Good stuff," Baebong says, stuffing more food into his mouth. He looks like someone suffering gonflay disease the way his cheeks are puffed out to the sides. "I haven't had an egg in forever."

"Me neither," I chime in. "Where'd you get them?" I look to Jeffers for the answer, a little worried about the expression I see there. "Don't tell me you have live chickens onboard." It's bad enough I missed a stowaway, but an entire roosting flock? There'd be no excuse for that.

"No," he answers, smiling, "we traded for some herbs. This will be the last of them before we do another deal."

"Speaking of deals," says Gus, "what's up with the dude in the holding cell?" He chews on a hard chunk of bread as he waits for my answer. His brother's jaw moves in tandem, giving me the strangest sensation that I'm suffering double vision. I have to look away to answer with any kind of focus.

"He says he makes deals." I shrug. "I've never seen him before, but Baebong has." I pick at the vegetables on my plate, not too excited about them. I'm too nervous to have the appetite I should, even though my plate holds fresh carrots and beans. These are traded almost like precious metals at most of the stations I've lived in. The problem is not the taste, of course. It's just me being in freak-out mode. My first ice-grab is less than five hours away, and I was never able to get much sim time for that operation. My stomach is once again in knots.

"We going to keep him?" Tam asks my lieutenant.

"Don't ask me. She's the boss." Baebong's fork waves in my general direction.

"Yeah, but you can vouch for him." Gus pushes. "Do you?"

"I'm not vouching for anyone. Can he do deals? Yeah. I saw him do that. Can we trust him? I have no idea." Baebong returns his focus to his plate, and I can tell from his body language that he's not interested in saying anything more. That's the thing about him: once he's said his piece, he's done. No amount of harassment on my part will get him to commit to anything else. I've tried on many occasions and failed every time.

"I say we give him a chance," says Gus. "We're short-crewed. We could use all the hands we've got."

"Tell you what," I say, leaning back in my chair. "Gus, you bring him some food, pick his brain a little, see what he's good for."

Gus nods slowly. "Okay. Yeah, I can do that. Recon. Maybe I'll test him a little. See if he knows what he's talking about."

I wipe my mouth off with the back of my hand. "Good. You do that, and I'm going to catch some sleep before the ice-grab." I stand and everyone rushes to follow suit.

I'm frozen in place, staring at the people around me. Everyone but our stowaway and Lucinda are present, and they're all waiting for me to say something. Never having sat at the captain's table myself, I have no idea what's expected of me.

"Uh. At ease?"

My crew takes their seats and continues with the meal like they didn't just completely rock my universe. I turn around, trying to act cool as I head for the corridor. *I did it, I did it, I did it! I acted like a captain and they bought it. Be cool, Cass, be cool.*

"You want me to show you to Langlade's old bunk?" Jeffers asks.

"No, that's all right," I say, stepping through the portal. "I saw it before on my tour."

I'm able to hold in my emotions until I'm around the corner, but then I just can't take it anymore. I let out a silent scream, my mouth wide open as I punch the air around me. *Yeah, baby! I'm the captain! Everybody stands at my table when I stand because they respect me!*

"A-hem." The sound of someone clearing her throat in front of me pulls me up short. My sudden-onset celebration turns into me attempting to appear as if I were trying to scratch an itch in the middle of my back.

"Oh, hey, Lucinda. Didn't see you there."

"I noticed." She moves to walk around me, but I step over to block her way.

"Where're you going?"

"Breakfast. Excuse me, please."

"Breakfast was served a half hour ago. You're late."

"I had things to do." She tries to move to the other side of the corridor, but I side-step, blocking her once more.

She sighs loudly and glares at me. "I'd like to eat, please. Could you move?"

"Nope. Breakfast is over."

She pulls herself up to her full height, which is just a few centimeters or so taller than me. "Excuse me?"

I stare her down. Or up, I guess. "Breakfast is served when I say it's served. You eat when I say you eat. If you can't get to my table on time, you either explain yourself, or you don't eat. That's the way it works around here now."

She laughs but then stops when she sees my expression. "You can't be serious."

"Of course I can." I smile.

"But Langlade let us eat whenever we wanted."

I take a small step back and look down at my feet, running my gaze up my own body and then back to her. "Do I look like Langlade to you?"

"No." Her jaw flinches. She's smart not to let the rest of the words on her mind fly.

"Good. Then there should be no confusion. I'm your new captain, and I require that all crew members report to meals when the food is ready and not later when they feel like it."

"This isn't a dictatorship."

I laugh. "Of course it is." I shake my head at her. "Since when have you ever flown on a ship run by committee?"

She shrugs. "We had a lot of freedom with Langlade."

"Yeah. So much freedom you had an entire biogrid growing under his nose without him being aware of it. Great idea. Where do I sign up for that?"

Her nostrils flare, but her voice remains calm. "Are you calling me a thief?"

"Not exactly."

"Well, I don't know where you come from, *Captain*, but around here, we don't appreciate being accused of things that sound like stealing."

I lean in and almost whisper my next thought. "Then maybe you shouldn't be doing things behind your captain's back anymore." I wink. "Catch you at lunch. Six hours from now. Don't be late." I shove past her and continue down the corridor with my hand at my thigh. If she jumps me, I'll be ready, but I won't turn around to see if she's coming. I've got too much pride for that.

"You can't starve me!"

"I don't plan to!"

"I'm going to get something to eat!"

"Not for breakfast you're not!" I stop at the nearest keypad and punch in the code for the dining room. "Jeffers!"

"Yes, Captain."

"Do not serve food to any latecomers. Not a single bite, you hear me?"

There's a long pause before his answer comes. "Okay."

"I have the monitors on, and I will know if you disobey." I turn up the volume on my voice a little so everyone in the dining room knows I'm talking to them. "And just so we're clear, anyone who disobeys me, floats. That's the deal. This is not a democracy, this is a dictatorship, and I'm the dictator."

"Can I give her my bread?" Gus asks.

"No. No one feeds latecomers. Those are the rules. Commit them to memory."

The last thing I need on this ship is people turning into loners and falling into Darksickness. A crew that eats together can make plans, read each other's moods, and be reminded of why they're doing what they do. A crew is a family, and family that shares meals together, stays together. That's what my grandpa used to say, anyway, and I have no reason to doubt his wisdom. I only wish my father had followed it more often.

I reach the entrance to my bunk and pass my hand in front of the keypad. The portal door slides open and I step through, inhaling the scent of Langlade and whatever perfumes he used to make himself smell more like an Earth tree than a man. It's not entirely unpleasant, but I'm still going to have the gingers run a vacuum filter cycle on this place. I need to sleep without distractions, and reminders of the guy who lost this ship to me, and the idea that he's probably not going to walk away as quietly as I would like, isn't going to cut it.

Falling onto the bunk fully clothed, I lie on my back and stare at the ceiling above me. Like just about every other part of the ship's skeleton, it's made of gray steeloid, smooth save for the bumps of laser weld that show up as small slivers of shadow. A warm, fuzzy light coming from glow-orbs along the edges of the room makes this surface appear almost soft and not the impossibly hard one I know it to be. I could almost call this place comfortable. I'm already feeling drowsy.

Now that I finally have a moment of peace to myself, I can find out what kind of onboard captain's assistant I have. I've never like the idea of depending on them much, all too familiar with the stories of rogue computer systems causing massive casualties on other ships in the past, but I wouldn't mind a second set of eyes on the place now that I know how easy it is to sneak on board and grow biogrids under the captain's nose.

I speak out into the chamber. "Computer, identify yourself."

There's a whir and a click before the answer arrives over the loudspeaker in my room. "I am known as Adelle."

"Adelle, I am your new captain. My name is Cass. This is my bunk. Do you understand?"

"I understand, but must verify your authority with our engineers."

I probably should have gone through this process of switching over command before, but sometimes that verification can take a long time —some of the computers on these older rigs still need a lot of hand-coding— and we didn't have that luxury at the station. It felt like Langlade was breathing down my neck, and I know his stupid pilot was ready to storm the ship. Leaving when we did was the right decision, I'm sure of it. But now I have to wait for the computer to switch over before we can do the ice-grab; it'll be too risky without Adelle's help.

"You do that, Adelle. And in the meantime, I'm going to take a nap. We have an ice-grab in five hours."

"Yes, Cass. I understand."

I can't keep the smile out of my voice, but it doesn't matter. Adelle won't hold it against me. She doesn't care that I haven't had a computer to do my bidding in three years. Three very *long* years.

"Adelle, wake me in four hours."

"Yes, Cass. I will wake you in four hours. I do not yet know your preferences. Would you like a harsh alarm sound or a soft one?"

"Start soft and see where that gets us."

"Yes, Cass. I will start with the soft alarm and only continue to the harsher ones if you do not respond. Is that correct?"

"Yep, that's correct." I barely get the words out before I'm falling asleep.

CHAPTER THIRTEEN

I SHOOT OUT OF BED like someone's set off a blast under my bed. And I'm pretty sure someone has, with the bomb detonations I hear going off around me.

"What the hell!" I scream, bringing my dagger up in front of me, even though I can barely see. My hair is completely covering my face. I quickly swipe it out of the way to ready myself for the imminent threat bearing down on me.

"Welcome back from your nap, Captain Cass." Adelle's voice is eerily soothing in the midst of the chaos.

I blink a few times, trying to figure out what the hell is going on.

"Uhh…" The glow-orb of realization starts to flicker and then burn in my brain. "Adelle?"

"Yes, Captain?"

I slowly sheath my knife as I realize there's no mutiny afoot complete with laser-loaded weapons and plasma rays. I've just been awakened from my nap as I requested.

"What in the hell was that?"

"That was your alarm, Captain."

"I thought we said we were going to start with the soft alarm first."

"Yes, you are correct. We did."

I sigh, realizing I'm dealing with an early generation device. My father's onboard compubots were so much more intuitive than Adelle seems to be. I can only imagine what her humanform kit looks like. Knowing Langlade, she'll have giant, malleable boobs. *So kinky. So gross.*

"I guess my idea of soft doesn't usually include bombs going off next to my head." I run my fingers through my hair, afraid to look in the mirror over Langlade's sink, but walking in that direction anyway.

"I started with a stringed instrument, worked my way through various droning engine noises and bells, and then finished with the wartime effects. You are a very heavy sleeper, Captain."

I stare at my reflection in horror. *What happened to my face? To my hair?* I look like a hundred-year-old woman who used her head to clean out an air duct during its yearly service. Using my fingers to untangle this nest is not going to get the job done. Searching the sink area, I find a comb and work with it as best I can to tame the beast that is my hair.

"I haven't slept in about three days," I say by way of explanation. Not that I need to do that. Adelle doesn't need my excuses. She has a job and she gets it done. Simple. Compubots are nothing if not efficient.

"That's not healthy, Captain. The human body needs at least six hours of REM sleep per twenty-four hour period to function at optimum levels."

"Yeah, well, tell that to my father," I say offhandedly. He loved getting me up after only four hours. Sleep deprivation was his greatest tool.

"Reaching First Major General Valemar Kennedy of the Omega Systems Group Defense Station, Elite Command."

"NO!" I scream, flipping the comb out of my hand in my panic. "Drop the reach! Drop the reach! Do not make that reach, Adelle!"

"Dropping the reach."

My heart is beating so hard, it feels like it's trying to escape my chest. And I don't blame it one bit. I don't want to be around for that contact either. I hate that this compubot knows who I am and how I'm connected to the rest of the universe. She obviously picked up my fingerprints from the keypads I've used and quickly made the connection through the OSG's public database. It's all part of her authentication process, of course. The one I told her to execute. I should have known this would happen, and hate that I was stupid enough to miss it.

"Holy shit, that was close." Sweat comes out of every pore on my body and mingles together to make big, fat droplets that slide down my skin and soak through my flightsuit.

"What was close, Captain?"

I grip the edges of the sink and lean into it, trying to gain control of my organic systems. I feel like I'm on the edge of a full breakdown. "Adelle, listen to me, and listen to me carefully, okay?" I have to breathe in and out a few times slowly before I can continue. "Do not ever, under *any* circumstances, make contact with that man. Do you understand?"

"My directive is to follow your every order to the letter."

"Good."

"And so if you order me to reach your father again, I must do as you say."

I drop my face into my hands. *Holy shit, what I wouldn't give for a live person some days.* "It was just an *expression*, Adelle. My overriding order that you should always follow is to never contact him in any case, in any situation, no matter what I say."

"You may change your mind. I must be able to adapt."

"I'm not going to change my mind. Believe me."

"Humans are incapable of remaining steadfast in the face of every adversity. There could come a time that you would change your mind. I need a codeword to override your latest order."

I have tried and failed to argue with an onboard computer before. So instead of trying to change this computer's pseudo thought processes, I humor it instead. "Fine, you want a code word? My code word is *asshole*."

"Noted. Your code word is asshole."

"No, wait. *Lying asshole*. That's the code: Lying asshole."

"Noted. Your code is lying asshole."

Memories churn in my head, getting me all fired up again. "Wait, it's not that; it's *lying sack of shit asshole*."

"That's a very long codeword."

I snort, still high on the anger my memories have conjured. "Yeah, but it's accurate."

"You are most likely to need your codeword during a period of great stress. In periods of great stress, humans are prone to forgetting longer codewords or phrases. Might I suggest you use a simpler version of this codeword?"

Adelle's right, I know she is. But I wish I could punch her in the face anyway. Maybe those malleable hooters will be good for something after all. Sometimes, nothing says 'Now you've *really* pissed me off' better than a good, old-fashioned boob punch.

"Fine. We'll just use asshole."

"Noted. Your override codeword is asshole."

And now that we have that under control, it's time to get down to business. I go back to trying to fix my hair. "Adelle, do whatever you have to do with the engineers to get me authenticated as captain. We'll need you for the ice-grab."

"I have already completed the authentication process. Your status as captain has been confirmed."

"And the ship's new name is the DS Anarchy, Adelle. Please change it in your systems."

"I have already done so, Captain."

"Excellent." I smile as the knot that was holding the right side of my hair hostage finally relinquishes its hold and allows the comb to slide through. A few more strokes later and it's smooth and shiny. Maybe a bit too shiny.

I lean in toward the mirror to see my reflection better. Then I look down at the comb and touch my fingers to the tines. They slide way too easily, and a residue remains on my fingertips.

"Goddammit." *Figures.* Langlade uses some kind of hair grease, and now I'm using it too. On one side of my head. *Perfect.*

Baebong's voice comes over the speaker. "Captain, this is Lieutenant So-Sun."

I smile at his formality. "Go ahead, Lieutenant."

"You ready to grab some ice? Gingers say we're a go."

"Yeah. I'll be up there in a couple minutes." I scan the room for some sort of grease remover, but the only thing that jumps into my line of sight is a hat. Knowing it's probably just as full of the grease as the comb, I give it a pass. The elastic I always keep in my pocket is going to have to do, and if anyone says anything about my ears, I'll just poke them with my knife.

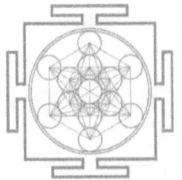

CHAPTER FOURTEEN

WHEN WE ARRIVE AT THE ice fields of Xylera, the flightdeck is full. Everyone but Tam and Rollo are up here with me, looking through the clearpanels at the gorgeous blue and white surface of the planet many drifters come to in order to replenish their water stores. As much as filtration science has advanced, we still can't seem to recapture all that we use, necessitating these runs from time to time. I hate that I'm still dependent on something outside my ship in order to exist, but life is what it is.

"That's not good," says Baebong, staring at a big war-ship hovering maybe fifty kilometers below us.

"What are they doing here?" Lucinda asks.

"I don't know," I say, kind of mumbling because my brain is racing to make sense of what I'm seeing. "Probably nothing good."

"Do warships do ice-grabs?" Jeffers asks.

"Not generally." I stare at the image of the WS and try to come up with a single reason why it would be here. "They use supply stations to take care of their water needs. I haven't seen one in years; not since the last uprising at Gartan."

"What were you doing on Gartan?" Gus asks, sounding impressed. It's not the nicest planet around, populated mostly by outlaws and shady businessmen.

"I happened to be on a cargo ship that was supplying food to some troops, and we landed there."

Gus shakes his head. "Seems like every ten years or so someone tries to make a grab for power."

"Yeah, but the OSG doesn't tolerate anyone taking that but themselves." My bitterness comes through in my tone, but I can't help it. I hate the OSG more than anyone I know. "We're lucky they've been content to colonize planets and set up the infrastructure to service them." It's the reason I'm flying a DS — so I can remain under their radar and live my life the way I want to and not how someone tells me I should. It's pretty much why anyone's a drifter, because living under a biodome or on a station can be a really easy life. When I lived with my father, I never went without ... unless he was holding something back to teach me a lesson, of course.

"Maybe they're just hanging out," Gus suggests, his tone telling me he doesn't believe that crap any more than I do.

"Bring 'em up on the comm," I say, sitting straighter in my chair. "Keep the visual off, though."

"Good call," Lucinda says.

I glare at her for a second because I don't need her approval or disapproval, but then go back to the clearpanel, listening as Baebong brings up the main frequency that begins to appear as he points the comm's directional beam at the WS.

"Warship, this is the DS Anarchy, twenty clicks aft and above. Over."

We hear nothing for several long seconds. Sweat trickles down my back.

"Warship, this is the DS Anarchy, twenty clicks aft and above. Over."

Another frequency lights up in red, blinking in the corner of the clearpanel.

"That's an emergency transmission," Jeffers says, pointing to it.

"Get me in," I say.

"On it," Baebong says, his hands flying over the controls.

Lucinda rests her hand on the arm of my chair, but I let her leave it there. I get the need for support right now. Our maiden voyage with me at the helm and we have a warship popping up and someone calling out an emergency. *What the hell? Who did I piss off in another life, anyway?*

"Hello, to the DS aft and above that warship, this is the DS Arcadia with an encrypted reach."

I nod to Baebong and he presses his comm button. "DS Arcadia, your reach is accepted." He selects the responding encryption passcode and puts it into place so we can hear the rest of his message. The emergency transmittor's tone changes to something a lot more sinister.

"Listen, that slimy bastard of a warship? It's trying to stop our ice-grab. Get out while you can."

I frown, looking at all my crew members in turn. *Halting their ice-grab? What does that even mean?* I take control of the comm knowing that nobody here has any more answers than I do.

"Arcadia, this is Captain Cass of the DS Anarchy. What in the hell are you talking about?"

"All I know is we're in mid-grab and they show up, telling us to shut it down so they can come aboard. Claiming rights to control water now? Fuck me, we're ass over aft down here. I suggest you get gone before they decide to shut you down too."

"But they have no right to do that!" I'm intimately familiar with the regulations concerning water rights on every single Dark Settlement of the Triangulum Galaxy. Water is free for everyone. The continuation of our species —something that was seriously in doubt after Earth was poisoned— depends on it.

"Yeah, we know. And yet, here they are. Listen, I've gotta go, but if you want help, go to the coordinates I'm transmitting now. Cutting comm in five seconds."

Five beats later and he's gone, and the next transmission we receive is from the warship.

"DS Anarchy, this is Warship Budapest. We acknowledge your transmission. State your purpose for being at Xylera."

What would a real captain do? Tell the truth? Lie? I look at my crew members, but they're all depending on me to handle this.

"My purpose is my business, Budapest, but I thank you for your concern."

Lucinda's hand slides off my chair and her arms cross as she stares out the clearpanel with everyone else. I take it as a positive sign. She looks tough, like she's not going to take any shit from this warship commander. I turn my attention back to the clearpanel and wait for a response. He doesn't make me wait long.

"Be advised, Anarchy, that as of this day we control all water extraction from Xylera and Haloid, so if that's part of your plan, we need to come onboard for an inspection and you'll need to pay the tariff."

"Inspection and tariff my ass," I say to my crew. To the Budapest, however, I smile and say, "Roger that, Budapest. We'll be on our way."

"What are you going to do?" Gus asks. "We need that water."

"Let's go find out what the Arcadia has for us, first." I look over at Baebong. "You have those coordinates dialed in?"

"Yep. All set."

"Bring us around the far side of Xylera. Don't go direct."

"Whatever you say, boss."

I look over at Jeffers and he's nodding, but not looking at me.

"What do you want me to do?" Lucinda asks. For the first time since I've met her, she doesn't sound pissed off. More like scared.

"Go talk to the guy we have in the holding cell. Rollo. He said something about changes coming. Find out if he knows anything about this." I gesture out the clearpanel at the Budapest.

"Okay."

As she heads for the door, I finish my thought. "And see what you can find on the biogrid to trade."

"Trade for what?" she asks, hesitating at the portal.

"Water."

Holy shit. My first full day, my first ice-grab, and suddenly the universe is changing on me? What are the odds of that happening? Hol-ee shit. I'm glad I got away from that givit table when I did.

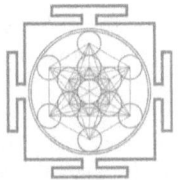

CHAPTER
FIFTEEN

FLYING AROUND THE DARK SIDE of Xylera is not a pleasant experience. Not because it isn't beautiful; the glow coming from the atmosphere reflecting the starlight is almost mesmerizing. The problem is that we have no idea if that warship is going to start following us and what we'll be able to do if it does. They can outgun, outrun, and outlast us any day of the year. The only thing they can't do is outmaneuver us. The only way to escape a warship determined to muscle us under is to dive down to a planet's surface and hide. I just wish I knew what the hell we were flying toward right now. I've never heard of the DS Arcadia before.

"How many minutes until contact?" I ask Baebong, tapping my finger next to the array panel.

"Five. What's the plan when we get there?"

"I don't know. Let's see what it is and then decide."

"It could be a landing spot," Jeffers suggests.

"Or a temporary trading station," Gus adds.

I nod. "Gus, maybe you'd better get to the engine room with Tam. Just in case."

"Just in case what?" he asks, his expression perking up.

"Just in case I need to fry someone, I don't know." Assuming they even have hot weaponry on board. I have to believe Langlade made sure of that.

He grins. "Excellent. Just call me when you need me." He jogs off the flightdeck, leaping from the top step almost all the way to the door.

"I think he likes blowing things up," I say, watching him go.

"He does," Jeffers says with a sigh. "It can be a problem sometimes."

I stare at Baebong's back. "I know the feeling."

Eight. That's how many fires Baebong has set in my living quarters over the past three years with one of his inventions. I have a feeling he and Gus are going to get along really well.

"I don't want to hear it," my lieutenant says without looking at me. Eyes in the back of his head, that guy has.

Jeffers looks at me with his eyebrows up, but I shake my head. Maybe around the dinner table we can talk about my bedroll catching on fire or my pack being vaporized, but not here. Not now. I need to figure out how to get some water and then get the hell out of here. The minutes blip by in what seems like slow motion.

The 'Talk' button lights up on my array and then Lucinda's face appears floating near it. I connect.

"Go ahead, Lucinda."

"I talked to Rollo." She grimaces. "He says he heard about the OSG shifting focus at the last station. Said there were rumors going around about ships being stopped and searched."

"Searched? For what?"

"No one knows. They're also claiming water rights, like they said."

"Bring him up, would you, please?"

"Yes." Her face disappears and the comm signal cuts off.

"Great." I shake my head, pissed I didn't spend more time in the dive bars while I was on that last station. That's where all the news is shared, not on the magnoscreens. I should have known better than to trust the shit disseminated by the OSG. Of course they wouldn't announce to the universe their plan to steal our basic human rights from us. That would cause an outright rebellion. Instead, they're hitting us one by one, when we're alone and weak. A totally classic move taken directly from their playbook. And I should know, because my father helped write the damn thing. *Bastards*.

"What are you thinking?" Jeffers asks. Baebong turns his chair to face me.

"I'm thinking that we need to do an ice grab where they don't have eyes, get our filtration systems as tight as we can, and then go lie low somewhere while this shakes out."

"I agree," Jeffers says. "Not that you need my agreement, Captain." He gives me a slight scolding look that has me rolling my eyes.

"Give it a rest, Jeffers. You know I had to nip that shit with Lucinda in the bud."

He nods once. "I realize you have a challenge on your hands."

"And?" Obviously he has more to say. I can't believe he's held back this much as it is.

"And Lucinda is … she can be…"

"A bitch?"

"No, I was going to say an ally. Or an enemy. Either way, she can be formidable."

"So you're saying it would be better if she were on my side."

"Yes. I am saying that. And I'm saying that out here in the Dark, drifting, one cannot have too many friends."

The idea of having a big group of friends makes my ass twitch, and not in a good way.

"Cass is more the loner type," Baebong offers. "Don't count on her for all that touchy feely stuff."

I scowl at him. "I can be touchy feely."

He snorts. "Yeah. Okay." His chair swivels and he goes back to monitoring our progress.

If I had something to throw, I'd aim it at his head, but since I don't, I just stare at the clearpanel. "How much longer?"

"We're here." Baebong presses some buttons. "Stop thrust."

I follow his instructions and then look at the view I have of the entire space around our ship. All I see is the Dark.

"There's nothing here."

Baebong points. "There! Cloaking device!"

I squint my eyes, seeing nothing. "You're dreaming. No one has a cloaking device that good." People have made efforts, but they might as well hang a glowing sign on their ship saying, 'Here I am! Over here!' the way it turns the space around them milky white. Something about the technology interferes with starlight or whatever. I'm not really much of a tech person, but Baebong is, and he should know better.

"Look there." Baebong throws a laser tack up on the clearpanel and uses it to draw a circle around something. "Warping. I can see it. Can't you?"

I can't, but I know when Baebong's excited, and this is as animated as I've seen him in a long time.

"Throw a beam at it." I wait, hunched over, as Baebong moves to follow my orders. Then I realize what could happen if we try to uncloak an unfriendly source.

"Wait!"

Baebong's finger hovers over the beam sending command.

Connecting into the engine room, I speak rapidly. "We have enough juice for a shield?"

"How big of a shield?" comes one of the ginger voices.

"Big enough for a warning shot."

"Yeah. But it won't leave us much after."

"We're using it. Be prepared for shit to hit the thruster blades."

I nod at Baebong. "Shield up and then beam it." I flip the all-comm switch and speak to the crew. "We're beaming and expecting a possible small hit. Shields are up, but put down any knives you might be carrying." The books are full of people stabbing themselves when gravitational equilibrium is lost.

Baebong's eyes go a little wide, but he moves to follow my orders. "Whatever you say, Ahab."

"Cass will do just fine." I grip the arms of my chair and brace for impact.

CHAPTER SIXTEEN

THE BEAM LEAVES THE DS Anarchy and spreads out to the spot Baebong claims he can see is cloaked. I half expect to see the ray disappear into the Dark, but when it doesn't, and instead lights up another DS in ghostly blue, I nearly piss my flightsuit.

"What in the name of all that is holy…?" I lean closer to the clearpanel, as if that will somehow dispel this illusion I feel as though I'm suffering.

Jeffers moves closer to the clearpanel. He sounds as incredulous as I feel. "That can't be. They're … cloaked."

Everyone talks about the ability to cloak a ship and hide from the OSG, but until now, it's always been relegated to that folder in my brain reserved for myths and wishes that will never come true.

"Told you." Baebong's hands hover over his array as he awaits my next order, while I chew on the inside of my cheek and try to figure out what the hell this all means.

"Post our channel," I say, worried if we try to transmit blindly we'll alert the warship to this other DS's presence. "Flash a landing light a few times so they know we can see them. Let them contact us."

The distinct glow of red lights comes around the clear-panel, reflecting off the protruding edges of our ship. It's quiet enough on the flightdeck now that you can hear each individual breath we're taking.

A crackling sound follows and then a glowing frequency number appears. "Reach encrypted," is all the voice says.

"Accepted," I say to the other DS and to Baebong.

He quickly selects the responding encryption passcode before it disappears, so we can hear the rest of the transmission. I can't wait for them to start talking; it feels like we're running out of time fast.

"Captain Cass of the DS Anarchy here. We see you but we don't see you. Over."

"DS Anarchy, this is Gunter Beltz, captain of the DS Mekanika. Someone on your ship has good eyes." His heavy Germanic accent has me smiling.

"That'd be my lieutenant. We received your position from the DS Arcadia. What's going on?" My palms are sweating. I try to wipe them dry on my flightsuit, but it doesn't work.

"Well, apparently, the OSG thinks it can control our water supply now. But we have something to say about that, do we not?"

"Yes, we do."

Jeffers is nodding off to my left, giving me the courage to continue.

"But how are we going to get our water without them seeing?"

Rollo and Lucinda appear through the portal and walk up onto the flightdeck, stopping next to my chair.

"What's going on?" Rollo whispers.

I wave him off so I can listen to Mekanika's response.

"We recommend a short-range grab," the guy says.

Rollo speaks softly. "Whoa. Sounds like Rollo picked the wrong DS to hitch a ride on."

"Are you sure there's no other way?" I ask.

"No. You can do it long range, of course, but then you must pay the tariff. I hear it is quite large."

I flip the comm switch for Gus and Tam. "Hey guys? Exactly how much water do we need to top off?"

Tam answers after a couple-second delay. "A megaliter, maybe? Give or take."

"Shit." I'm back to chewing the inside of my cheek. "That's not good."

"What's not good?" This is Gus speaking, now. I can tell by the slightly carefree vibe to it.

"We're being told to do a short-range grab."

"Awesome. I hope we don't die."

A fainter voice comes over the comm. "Did she say we might die? Did I hear that right?"

"Shut up," Gus says to his brother. "Just get that up-take config fixed. We need it."

"Fixed?" My heart flips over in my chest cavity. "Did you say he needs to fix something?"

"Yeah, but it's no big deal. Just relax. He'll have it good in no time."

"No, I won't!" comes the fainter voice. *Tam.* "I'm missing a part!"

"Goddammit!" I shout, banging my fist on the arm of the chair.

"What part does he need?" Baebong asks. Then he presses his own comm button. "What part do you need, Tam?"

"Oh, nothing," he says sarcastically, "just a boom chuck."

"A boom chuck? That's what keeps the boom from hitting the ship, right?" I look around the room, hoping someone is there to tell me I'm wrong.

"Yep," Rollo says. "Could-a scored you one of those at the last station. All you had to do was ask Rollo." He lets out a long-suffering sigh, which I ignore.

I link up comm with the other DS. "Mekanika … any chance you have a spare boom chuck for a DS lying around?"

Lucinda laughs bitterly behind me.

A crackling over the speaker precedes the answer. "As a matter of fact, our stock in trade is DS parts. You need the standard boom chuck or the Mekanika upgrade?"

I feel like I could fly outside without a darksuit right now, I'm so high on life. *What are the chances we'd need a part and then end up floating right next to a hardware trader? Maybe the universe doesn't hate me after all.* Now I just need to figure out what a Mekanika upgrade is without looking like an idiot.

Baebong shrugs when I look to him for an explanation. After quickly connecting the engineers to my open line to Mekanika, I ask my next question.

"What's the difference between a regular boom chuck and a Mekanika version?" *Might as well call a spade a spade. I'm an idiot.*

"Mekanika version is lighter and self actualizing. No need to give a manual hitch."

"I want it," Tam says in a rush. "Get me that one."

I point at Rollo. "You go talk to the gingers and get a list of what they need. Everything. Your job is to acquire all that stuff at the next station."

He looks at me kind of funny. "You got money? Because a boom chuck ain't cheap."

I look at Lucinda. "I have something better than money."

Her chin lifts in the air and she turns away, but not before I see the flash of pride in her eyes.

"We'll take the Mekanika special," I say. "Are you prepared to be boarded under that cloak?"

"No, I am sorry, but we are not. I can shoot the package out to you. What do you have to trade?"

"You don't want credits?" I can't believe our good fortune.

"No. We would like a dead chicken, please."

My jaw drops open.

Baebong speaks before I can. "What the fuck is up with the dead chicken, action, man?"

CHAPTER
SEVENTEEN

IMOTION FOR JEFFERS TO come closer as Rollo leaves to talk to the gingers. Lucinda moves in without my invitation. I mute the comm with Mekanika so we can have a private flightdeck conversation.

"What's up with the dead chicken? Seriously."

They both shrug.

"I have no idea," Lucinda says.

"Me either." Jeffers looks over at Baebong. "You said you incinerated it?"

"Hell yeah, I incinerated it. Who keeps a dead chicken lying around?"

Everything keeps swirling around in my head, and I'm having a hard time keeping it straight. *The OSG controlling our water? A cloaked DS that makes custom parts? Dead chickens being used to barter? What the hell.* None of this kind of crap played out on the simulator or in the manuals I studied and practically memorized.

I connect back up with the other DS, hoping I'm doing the right thing. "We used to have a dead chicken."

We wait, holding our collective breath, for his response.

"What did you do with your dead chicken, may I ask?"

"Well," I try to laugh it off, "heh-heh, it kind of stunk so we incinerated it."

There's a long pause before he answers.

"That is unfortunate."

We all exchange confused glances. I lean toward my array as I speak. "And why is that?"

"Go check your incinerator and maybe you will see."

Baebong and Lucinda take one look at one another and then scramble from the room, leaving me with Jeffers.

"We'll get right back to you," I say, before muting the connection again. "What do you think he means by that?" I look to our ship's cook and healer, knowing he doesn't have the answer I seek.

"I wish I knew."

"Do you think there was something inside the chicken?"

"It sounds like that might be the case."

"But why a chicken?"

Jeffers thinks about it for a few seconds before responding. His eyes have a faraway look to them. "In some communities, the chicken is a very rare commodity. Perhaps if you kept a dead chicken, it wouldn't be considered all that strange to someone who knows this."

I think about my past life, how I used to have chicken several times a week. I never wondered much about where they came from or the fact that others didn't have that luxury. That's the danger of living too close to the OSG; you become blind to what the rest of the universe must do to survive.

I think about the stench that was in the former pilot's bunk. "I suppose a dead chicken would be the last place someone in the OSG would go looking for something important."

"Or valuable," Jeffers adds.

We both go silent as we consider the ramifications. *Was there something important hidden in the pilot's room? Is that why he came after us both on the dock and then in that PS, risking being turned into space junk with the way he was flying it?* Baebong said there wasn't anything left in his bunk besides the chicken. That must have been what he was coming back for. *But why didn't he take it when he left for his appointment with the prostitute?*

There are too many mysteries on this ship for my liking or comfort. As soon as we can bed down somewhere without interference, I'm doing a full sweep and having a come-to-captain meeting with all the crew. But for now, I need to find out what the hell is going on with dead poultry and a cloaked DS offering me the one thing I need to survive out here.

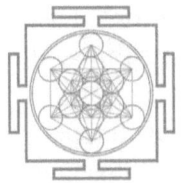

CHAPTER EIGHTEEN

BAEBONG COMES BACK ONTO THE flightdeck fifteen minutes later with Lucinda right behind him.

Seeing something in the palm of his hand, I stand. "What is it?"

He comes up the stairs with his hand out. There's a flat, black disk there with no identifying markings on it at all that I can see.

"I have no idea what it is or how damaged it got in the fire," he says, a little breathless. If the look in his eyes is any indicator, he's itching to get the thing on his workbench so he can figure it out.

Taking it from him, I run my finger over the top of it. Some soot comes off, but the surface of the thing itself seems undamaged. It's black, shiny, and very slightly rounded toward the centers. "Fire safe," I say mostly to myself.

"Hard as hell, too," Baebong says. "I scratched the wall with it on the way in."

"What'd you do that for?" I ask.

"I asked him the same thing," Lucinda says, rolling her eyes.

"To test its density, of course." He shakes his head at us non-engineering types. "Stronger than steeloid, at least."

"Are we going to trade it?" Jeffers asks.

I shake my head. "No. If it's so important he'll trade that big boom part for it, and that nutcase pilot came after us for it, I think we need to keep it and figure out what it is before we decide to hand it over to someone else."

"But he said he wants it," Jeffers says. "And we can't do a short-range grab without his boom chuck."

"He'll just have to trade for something else." I look to our biogrid creator. "What do you say, Lucinda? Do you have something he might want?"

She shrugs. "Maybe. You'll have to ask him."

I look at my crew members one at a time before speaking to them. "Are we in agreement that we don't give him the device in trade? That we keep its existence secret for now?"

"Why are you asking us?" Lucinda says. "I thought this was a dictatorship."

My knife hand is getting very twitchy. "It is. But that doesn't mean I don't value your opinions."

She looks like she's going to be stubborn about it, but then when she glances at Jeffers and he nods, her shoulders relax.

"I'm in agreement," Jeffers says.

"Me too," Baebong chimes in.

I wait for Lucinda, staring at her but not being aggressive about it. We're on the dark side of Xylera; I can wait all day for her to stop being a pain in the ass if I have to.

"Fine. I agree." She turns around and heads for the portal.

"Where are you going?" I ask, watching her leave.

"To do some inventory. See what we might be able to offer."

Relief floods through me. At least for now, Lucinda is on my side. "Good." It's like a pendulum with her, first she despises me, then she supports me. I'm going to have to deal with her later.

Walking over to my chair, I make myself stop worrying about Lucinda's split personalty so I can focus on what I'm going to say to Captain Beltz of the DS Mekanika. It's generally frowned on to outright lie to another DS captain, but a small fib is easily overlooked. *How much to reveal and how much to conceal?* That's always the question when you're dealing in the Dark.

"Captain Beltz, this is Anarchy. We didn't find anything in the incinerator. What exactly are we looking for? Chicken bodies don't hold up well under the heat."

There's a long pause before he comes back to us. I'm almost ready to worry about being shot at when he does finally answer.

"Are you certain? You did not find anything quite small and perhaps dark in color?"

My ears begin to burn with the lie, but I ignore it and focus on keeping my voice even. "No, sorry. There wasn't much in there, since we offloaded our waste at a station just a few hours ago. But we have some things we got in trade from a biogrid." Better that he doesn't yet know we are the actual owners of the biogrid at this point. Not until I get his measure.

"Hmmm, I don't know. We are pretty well stocked here."

"Anything exotic or crazy you don't have that you might want? Some tea maybe?"

I hold my breath as I wait for his answer.

"How about … you got any nuts onboard there?"

Are you kidding? That's all we have onboard The Anarchy.

"I'm not exactly sure. Let me check."

CHAPTER
NINETEEN

I TAKE THE POSSIBLE TRADE inventory list from Lucinda and read the items I can stand to part with out loud over the comm to the captain of the DS Mekanika, my eyes widening as I take in all the entries.

"Okay, Captain, we have available for trade... three kilos of hazelnuts, five kilos of shelled peanuts, and a half kilo of cashew nuts." *Who knew? We are loaded with nuts on this ship, crew not included.*

"Yes, you do have some nuts, don't you? Where did you get all of those things?" He sounds way happier than I'd be about the situation. Maybe I had too many of them when I was younger. We always had bowls of them sitting out on tables for anyone to munch on when they were visiting.

"A trade the former owner of this thing made before I got her. I don't have the details. You interested?"

"Yes, we are very interested. Please come to the trade hatch, and we will make the switch."

"Standard protection protocol?" I ask, hoping he'll say yes. I have no idea what equipment this ship has onboard for heightened security during a trade.

"Yes, of course. We are all friends." He chuckles after this, which doesn't make me feel comfortable at all.

I mute the comm so I can give instructions without Beltz listening in.

"Make sure we don't short him," I say to her.

Baebong takes his seat at the console and Lucinda heads for the door.

"If anything, give him a little extra. I have a feeling we're going to need a lot of parts, so he's a good friend to have out here."

"Yes, Captain," she says before disappearing through the door.

This time I don't detect any sarcasm in her tone. I'm two for two with her. I tell my brain to stop spinning over the idea that I actually might have earned some respect from her today, but it doesn't want to listen.

"I'm going to get you a drink of water," Jeffers says, looking at me funny.

"I'm fine," I say, just as another wave of dizziness hits me. I sit down hoping to play it off like it's nothing. My eye falls on the black disk sitting on Baebong's station array. My crazy mind is blaming that stupid thing for the headache that's starting to blaze up in the back of my head. *I was fine until that thing came up on the flightdeck, wasn't I?*

"It's easy to get dehydrated out here," he says, ignoring my claim of good health. "Be right back."

Baebong hits his comm button. "Gus and Tam, we're readying for a trade, standard protocols. We all good with that?"

"All good," one of them says. I'm too tired to suss out which one. "You have an ETA?"

"Fifteen minutes," I mumble. I planned to say it loudly so they'd hear me over the sounds of the engines that are cranked up in the background, but my words come out slurred for some reason.

"Fifteen minutes," Baebong says louder, glancing at me over his shoulder and frowning. "That enough time?"

"Sure. We're just twiddling our thumbs down here. Nothing to see." That one was Gus. I may not have known him for very long, but that tone in his voice makes my ass twitch.

"Grab the extinguisher!" yells Tam from somewhere nearby.

I sit up straighter.

"Shut up, dick!" This is said with a hand attempting to muffle the comm-out.

"Extinguisher?" Baebong asks, turning his chair slowly to look at me as we wait for the answer.

"Rollo's got it!" comes Rollo's voice over the speaker.

"Nah, he's just messing around," Gus says to us, laughing too loudly.

The distinct sounds of fire-suppression foam shooting out at high velocity come over the comm next.

"Go see what's going on," I say to Baebong, sighing as I lean back in my chair and stare at the ceiling.

"You need help with the trade, though."

"Nah, I'm good. Just go. Jeffers will be back soon."

And that's the last thing I remember before waking up in my bunk with three faces hanging over me.

CHAPTER
TWENTY

I STARE UP AT JEFFERS, Rollo, and Lucinda, disori-
ented and sick to my stomach as I lie on my back in my
bunk.

"What...?" I croak out, trying to sit up.

Jeffers pushes my shoulder down and my body col-
lapses beneath the puny force. "Just rest. You shouldn't
get up yet."

Searching the faces above me gets me nowhere. All I
see is concern and worry, and not all of it's focused on me.
Lucinda keeps looking over her shoulder toward my door.

"What's going on? What happened to me?"

"We're about to find out," Jeffers says mysteriously.

The comm speaker at my door lights up, and Tam's
voice comes out over it. "Captain Beltz is aboard. I repeat,
Captain Beltz of the DS Mekanika has come aboard."

"What?!" I sit up just fine this time, functioning under the righteous energy that comes from being boarded by a possible enemy in the middle of nowhere Xylera. *How dare they let a stranger onboard my ship! That's mutiny!*

"Easy, now," Jeffers soothes, "he's here to help."

"Help with *what?*"

"We'll talk about it when he gets here. We're not really sure."

Rollo and Lucinda enter into a private conversation across the room I can't hear.

I growl in a low voice at Jeffers. "Who in the hell authorized his access onto my ship?"

"Your second in command." Jeffers gestures at Baebong. "You were incapacitated, and he had to make the call. But for what it's worth, I think it was the right one."

A booming at my door interrupts the rest of what Jeffers might have wanted to say. Someone who doesn't know how to use the very simple ringer on the keypad is here, and my guess is he has a massive fist. It sounds like we're being blasted by a particle ray when he pounds on the door a second time.

A deep voice comes through the steeloid like the thing is made of celluloid paper. "Come out, come out, wherever you are!" This is followed by a maniacal giggle that makes the little hairs on my butt stand up.

"What have you done?" I growl at my crew members and the stowaway.

"Rollo didn't do anything," Rollo says, holding up his hands in surrender. "He's just here for the show."

"Shut up, idiot," hisses Lucinda. "You're the one who suggested we get him involved."

"Involved?" I look at Jeffers. "Involved in what?" *They wouldn't really have invited him on the ship without my say so, would they have? As soon as I was down they took on a new captain?* My heart hurts just thinking about it. I'm being such a chick right now, but it's impossible to ignore the fact that I feel cheated on. And if he tries to take my seat on the flightdeck, I'm going to have to stab him. This is not a good day at all.

Jeffers ignores my question. "Go let him in."

Rollo walks away to do as he's told, and the room falls silent. I glare at Jeffers and then Baebong.

"There's going to be hell to pay for this later," I say to both of them.

"Please reserve judgment until it plays out." Jeffers remains calm in the face of my threat, which only serves to piss me off more. He should fear me more than he does. I'm going to have to rectify that shortcoming in his personality very soon.

The door is open suddenly, to a hulking man of about two meters. I guess him to be in his early thirties, maybe a little older. He squeezes through the doorframe of my room and enters the small space, commanding it with his mere presence.

"So, what do we have here?" he says in his funny accent. "A little girl by the look of it. OSG offspring, maybe?"

My heart freezes in my chest. No more beats come to circulate my blood through my veins. *Damn, that hurts.*

"What do you mean?" Lucinda asks, glaring at me with suspicion again. So much for earning her trust. The pendulum has swung to the other side and now she hates me again. *Fickle bitch. Oh well. Shit happens.*

His focus shifts to Jeffers. "Did you put the disk back inside the chicken like I instructed?"

"No, we don't have a chicken."

"But you have the disk, yes?"

No one says a word, but the guilt on their faces tells him everything he needs to know.

"Well, I can see you put it somewhere far from this girl, at least. That is why she is awake." He comes over and goes down on one knee to rest at my side. His face looms large just centimeters from mine. "How are you feeling? A little woozy maybe?" He has a huge grin on his face that I'd love nothing more than to slap right off. Unfortunately, my arm feels like it's made of steeloid; I can't lift it from the bed.

"Why does that make you so happy?" I ask, pissed about the whole thing. Somehow I got whammied, but I have a very hard time believing it has anything to do with that chicken disk.

He cocks his head first one way and then the other. "Well, I am happy because it means two things: one, that my cousin's invention is working, and two, that we found a little OSG spy right here in our middle." He reaches out and pokes me in the nose. "And a very cute one, too. I will enjoy watching you float."

"Float?" I swing my way-too-heavy legs over the side of the bed. "You're insane." At least my arms seem to be back to their normal weight. I flex my hand, wrist, and then elbow just to be sure.

He reaches out to push me back, but I grab his hand and pull his arm toward me. With my other hand, I take my knife out and hold it at the artery that runs up the base of his thumb.

Lucinda gasps and Jeffers steps back.

"Whoa, dude," Rollo says. "She's fast with that knife. Did you see that? Rollo didn't see it 'til it was right there on his wrist."

I stare Beltz down so he knows I'm not playing around. "Never touch me without getting my permission first."

Rollo whispers to Lucinda, "Not the touchy feely type, I guess."

"Why does everyone keep saying that?!" I yell. "I can be very touchy feely! Sometimes!"

Beltz tries to pull away, but I press the knife into his skin, drawing a very fine line of blood from it. The teeth on the back side of my blade will rip his skin off if he tries to yank his hand from my grip, and he knows it, so he stays put. He nods and smiles again.

"You are a crazy little girl, you know that?"

"So I've been told," I growl at him. "Now back the hell up so I can get off this bed and onto my feet."

Everyone in the room moves as far away as possible as I follow his motions in reverse, taking care to leave the knife in place at his wrist. It's not the best bleed point, but I'd never get my dagger up to his neck without climbing up on a box or something first. This little threat of mine is the only way I know I can stay safe with this giant of a man bent on sending me out the airlock without a darksuit on. I've never used a wrist cut as an intimidation technique before, but hey, it's working, and a girl's gotta do what a girl's gotta do.

"Here's what's going to happen," I say, once I'm solidly on my feet. The dizziness has almost completely passed, and thankfully my legs don't feel ten times their normal weight anymore. "You're going to turn around and head up to the flightdeck. Once we're there, you're going to submit to being restrained while we have a little conversation about that chicken thing and why you're on my ship."

Jeffers moves to the door and opens the portal for us. Lucinda and Rollo practically scamper out of it and disappear down the corridor. The echoes of their boots going in fast forward ring around the room, fading as they get farther away.

"I'm here because your crew invited me." He stares down at me, from almost a half meter higher. I'm not too proud to admit he's intimidating as hell with that crewcut blond hair, deepest blue eyes, and neck as thick as one of my thighs.

"I said we talk on the flightdeck, not here."

His nostrils flare at my orders. Then his gaze flickers, telegraphing his intent a full second before he follows through on it. He thinks he's going to get one over on me, but I'm ready for him, having practiced this move only about three thousand times in the past fifteen years.

His free hand shoots out to grab me by the back of the neck, and I've no doubt he could snap it with one squeeze of those meaty fingers. My knife hand leaves his artery and makes a quick slicing motion at his approaching arm, catching him in the bicep. My razor-sharp blade cuts through his flightsuit like it's made of air.

"Gottverdammt!" he roars, grabbing at his flayed and bleeding skin, his plan to grab me forgotten in the wake of his pain and blood loss. Injuries suffered in the Dark are serious. Without the right medications or MI equipment, a person could die from something like this, and he knows it.

Taking advantage of his pain and surprise, I leap forward and press the tip of the blade into his flight suit over his heart. I let it prick his flesh a little, just in case he's thinking about getting the stupid idea to fight me again. Out of the corner of my eye I see Jeffers holding his heart, his face a weird, almost gray color.

Standing flat on my feet, ready for anything, I glare up at Beltz, adrenaline making my pulse go crazy. I can hear it pounding in my skull. Using the calmest voice possible, I lean in toward him so he can hear me loud and clear. "Touch me without my permission again, Beltz, and I'm going to spear your fucking heart, cut it out of your chest, and eat it for dinner."

He stares down at me for what feels like a really long time. His expression goes from mutinous, to confused, to accepting, and then amused. Finally, he relaxes his posture, his shoulders going down and his weight shifting over to one foot, and the threat vibe I felt coming from his bad attitude dissipates into nothing.

"I change my mind about what I said earlier," he says. His eyes are practically sparkling. I'm not sure how it's possible, but he looks happy about the fact that I just sliced him open and threatened to cannibalize his body. Other men from my past finding themselves in a similar situation were more interested in shooting me glares of pure evil at this point. It makes me want to know more about this Beltz character and what makes him tick. *Keep your friends close and your enemies closer*. My father's words ring uncomfortably in my ears.

"Oh yeah?" I ease back on the blade a little, my nerves making me twitchy. I'm worried I'll cut him by accident if I'm not careful. It's not in my nature to hold back once I get started.

"Yes. You are not a crazy little girl. You are a crazy bitch." He grins so hard I'm nearly blinded by his big, white teeth.

I pull the knife away and put it back in its sheath, no longer worried he's going to try anything. I've known guys like him for years. They have two speeds: kill and let live, and we just downshifted out of the danger zone. "Just remember that about me and we'll be fine."

He reaches out with his uninjured arm and claps me on the shoulder. If I didn't know any better, I'd think some-one just dropped a sledgehammer on me.

"Okay, I will remember. Now, tell me… why does the schlafhammer work its magic on you, crazy bitch?"

I give him a wry look. "You can just call me Cass. And what in the hell is a schlaf-whatever?"

"Schlaf*hammer*. The 'sleep hammer', in English. It is the disk we keep inside the chicken."

I shrug. "How am I supposed to know? I don't even have a schlaf…"

"Hammer," he fills in for me. "Schlafhammer. It only works on members of the OSG. All those slimy little devils who have the OSG picochip in their bodies."

"Chip? What chip?" Chills move up and down my spine. I don't know anything about any chips, but I don't like where this is headed.

"You're OSG? Seriously OSG?" Lucinda is back in my doorway, Rollo standing behind her, prepared to use her as a shield if necessary, the coward. Her accusation bites into my skin.

"No, don't be ridiculous." I'm tempted to spit in disgust, but this is my room, so I don't. "Never in a million years."

Lucinda's not buying it; I can tell by the look on her face. "Then why does that schlephammer thing work on you and not us?"

"*Schlaf*hammer," Beltz says, rolling his eyes. "It's not that difficult. Try it. You can say it."

"Shut up," Lucinda says, not even looking at him. All her attention is on me. "You should have told us you were OSG before we agreed to continue on with you."

"Why would I tell you something that's not true?" I look first at her and then Jeffers. "Believe me, I'm not

OSG. Is my family OSG? Yes. Okay. Fine. But that doesn't matter. They're not on this ship, and they don't know I'm here, so it doesn't matter."

Lucinda finally looks at Beltz. "You said she has a chip."

He shrugs. "I assume, yes. She is sick, is she not?"

I shake my head, staring at the floor. Trying to concentrate with all these people crowding my room while still suffering the aftereffects of whatever hit me is impossible. "This is crazy."

"You should let me take a look at that injury," Jeffers says to Beltz, referring to his bicep. There is quite a bit of blood on his flightsuit now. "Before you go back to your ship."

"You are a healer?" Beltz asks, suddenly interested in something other than me.

"Of a kind."

"Oh, that is good news. Okay, I will come with you." He looks at me. "You go to my ship. Ask my cousin Jens to scan your body for the chip. Then we will know."

"What?" This is making no sense to me at all.

Rollo rubs his hands together. "Can Rollo go? Rollo loves visiting new ships."

"Yeah," I say, bitterly, "we noticed."

"One escort. I will allow that. But not him." Beltz flicks his gaze at Rollo before he turns and heads for the door, Jeffers leading the way. He looks back at me and winks. "You want the chip to stay or go? We can remove it for you, if you want."

With every word that leaves his stupid lips, my crew doubts me more. My words come out staccato as I try to control my anger. "I *don't* have a *chip*."

"Okay. If you say so." He chuckles as he goes out the portal and into the corridor beyond, following Jeffers' lead.

"I'm going with you to do that scan," Lucinda says, sounding like she expects me to argue.

"Fine." I shove past her and Rollo as I head to the airlock that will allow me to board the DS Mekanika. If Lucinda wants to come and watch, she can come, but I'm not waiting for her distrusting ass.

CHAPTER
TWENTY-ONE

I DON'T KNOW WHAT I was expecting exactly, but this isn't it. The DS Mekanika is so clean, it gleams. It makes the Anarchy look like a station toilet in comparison. I make a mental note to demand a full clean-up by the entire crew when I return. *If I return.*

A large man even bigger than Beltz is waiting for us as we enter the cargo bay of the DS Mekanika through our connected airlocks.

Thumbs hooked into the waistband of my flight suit, I nod at him. "I'm Cass, Captain of the DS Anarchy."

"I know who you are," he says simply. And then he turns, expecting Lucinda and me to follow. Apparently, the introductions are over.

"I didn't catch your name," I say, taking long strides to try and keep up with him. His back is rapidly disappearing down the corridor. Lucinda is already getting breathless behind me.

He doesn't answer. Instead, he stops outside the door that on my ship is the engine room. He bangs on it, ignoring the keypad that would be a much more subtle announcement of our arrival. The echoes of his fist booming on the door ring out around us. Apparently, it's a thing with these beast-men not to use keypads; they'd rather rattle the portal doors off their tracks.

A face appears in the window. The boy inside looks like he's about twelve. When he sees us standing there, his eyes go wide and then the door slides open.

"Wow. You're not what I was expecting," he says. Then he grins.

"I know what you mean," I say wryly. *A child is going to mess with my body? I don't think so.*

The smattering of bristles on his chin tells me he's older than twelve, but no way is he my age. Too many zits for that. I wonder why he doesn't do what everyone else his age does, namely visit a med station somewhere and have his hormones adjusted to make those angry-looking bumps disappear. Maybe he's one of those originists who doesn't believe in all the modern medical technology used to make us more visually appealing.

I have to admit, I'm not much of a fan of MI either. The more those people stick me with things, the less I like the idea of medical intervention. It has always struck me as cheating and inviting things in that should stay outside of everyday life. I've seen enough MI addicts to know I'd rather not avail myself of its temptations — the perfect face, the perfect body, skin that hardly ages. Sure, ridding the universe of cancer and earth-borne viruses and all those horrible diseases is nice; but the stuff they do these

days —changing people's faces, skin color, body shape—
it's going too far. Too much. That's the problem with humans; they always want to go beyond the limits and then
realize only when it's too late that they can't turn back.

"So you're the OSG spy, huh?" He backs away from the
door and gestures for us to enter. "Come on in. My name
is Jens. I spell it with a J, but you say it like a Y. *Yens*. It's
Germanic. My cousin's first name is Gunter. Our family
traces back to Germany on Earth."

Talk about too much information. I have no idea why some
people take so much pride in tracing their roots back to a
specific spot on Earth. The place is a wasteland now, every square centimeter of it — poison for all humans who
approach. There is no more Germany, no more America,
no more Africa; it's all gone. Only those who were living on the twenty-three space stations during the last war
survived, and now here we are nearly two hundred years
later: some half a million souls trying to survive out in the
Dark. At least the only alien life we've encountered so far
is plant-based and bacterial.

"I'm not a spy," I say, working to keep a short rein on
my temper. This kid is supposed to be able to prove my
innocence, so it wouldn't be smart to piss him off. He'd
better not expect me to dump all my family history on him
as part of this process, though.

"Then why'd you get sick when the disk was on your
ship?"

"I have no idea what you're talking about. We don't
have a disk. Just do this scan or whatever and then we'll
be on our way."

He pulls a stool out from under a workbench that's covered in mechanical parts. "Have a seat." Busying himself
with a box and its attached wand, he whistles. I recognize

the tune but can't place it. It's been a while since I've had access to music.

Glancing over at the door, I see the hulking form of our escort there, his arms crossed, his jaw set, and his stance saying we aren't going anywhere until he decides. His hair is blond, although a darker version of Beltz's and Jens's. Deep-set eyes make him seem sinister, and his emotionless attitude does nothing to dispel that vibe. I think he'd sooner slice me from stem to stern than look at me for much longer. I suddenly have the urge to get the hell out of there, but just as I'm about to stand, Lucinda glares at me.

"What?" I ask, leaning back on the stool a bit, acting like I'm perfectly comfortable being on show for these idiots.

"I can't believe you didn't tell us."

I throw my arms up, beyond frustrated. "There's nothing to tell! I'm not OSG!"

Jens is at the table, his wand moving over three tiny picochips on the bench. I recognize them as the same type we used in personal comm devices around our wrists during training when I was between the ages of ten and fifteen, before I advanced to the elite corps and before I left my father's rule for good. The device around his neck beeps each time the wand moves over one of them. I wish I could see them better from where I'm sitting, to determine if there's some sort of identifier imprinted on their capsules, but I'm too far away.

The wand comes up in Jens's hand as he spins around to face me, and stops right in front of my nose, ending my attempts at learning more about the picochips. Trying to bring the thing into focus makes my eyes cross.

"Just let me adjust the sensitivity," he says absently, turning some dials on the box he has affixed around his neck with a strap. I close my eyes as he looks down and accidentally bonks me in the nose with the device.

"Oh, sheisse, sorry." A few more turns of his dials and a squealing comes out of the front of it. "Whoa, too much." Dialing it back, he finally looks up at me. "Ready?"

I shrug. "Ready for nothing to happen, yeah."

He starts up at the top of my head, frowning in concentration. He looks down from time to time at his readout, managing to tap me on the head every time he isn't focused on what he's doing with the wand.

"Do you mind?" I ask, sighing loudly.

"Mind?" He looks up and sees his machine resting on my chin. "Oh, sorry. Still getting the hang of this thing." He lifts it off and moves it behind first one ear and then the other. Nothing happens, of course.

"Looks like they didn't put it in your brain at least. That's a good sign."

I shake my head. "You're completely insane. You actually believe my family would put a chip in my head?" My dad's an asshole, but he always prized my intellect. He wouldn't have let anyone mess with my gray matter.

He shrugs. "I've seen it. The machine doesn't lie." He goes back to his readout, tapping me on the side of the face with his wand in the process.

"How long is this going to take?" Lucinda asks. "I have things to do."

"Like pack your bags?" I ask sarcastically. One small sign that things aren't going how she likes, and she's all ready to throw in the towel. So much for crew loyalty. At least I know better than to trust her in the future. She's already shown she'll turn on me with very little provocation.

It's positively depressing, really. So far, being a captain of a DS is nothing like I imagined it would be. Of course,

I had thought all along that more of my friends would be joining me. That would have made a difference, I'm sure. But they chose to stay behind and continue to live hand to mouth, preferring an existence of knowing they had nothing to one of hoping they could have more some day and working toward making that hope a reality. *Oh well. At least now I know who my real friends are.* Or friend, singular. *Baebong.* I hope he's not planning on taking off on me. I wasn't exactly very open about my origins with him either. At the time, it seemed perfectly reasonable to keep my history out of the equation, but now I'm doubting my decision to stay completely anonymous from everyone in my life.

"Shouldn't take too long if she's clean," Jens says, answering Lucinda's question.

"I'm clean." I nearly growl at him, I'm so frustrated.

"We'll see." The wand moves down to my chest, bumping into my left boob.

I slap his hand away. "Watch it, perv."

He looks up shocked and then his face goes really red. "Oh, sorry. That was an accident."

"Sure it was." I glare at him, knowing he sees women maybe once every few months. "Just keep your paws to yourself."

"All right, ease up, I said I was sorry." He shakes his head and goes back to his machine, but his face is really red.

Hmm. Another virgin, perhaps? A kindred spirit? We are a very rare breed.

"How old are you, anyway?" I ask, curious now about who he is and how he got to be here on this ship making detection devices. I've seen a few young people on crews over the years, but he's much younger than any I've known who can actually make things like this machine he's using.

"Fifteen. How about you?"

"Nineteen."

His wand moves to my stomach. "Your family is OSG?"

"Yes." My own face goes red at the admission. "But I don't have any contact with them whatsoever." I say this for Lucinda's benefit, although I don't look at her to see if she's paying attention. "Not for years."

"We'll see," he says, running the wand down the front of my legs.

When he reaches my feet without his device sounding off, I smile. "See? No chip. Told you so."

"Stand up, please," he says, giving a wry smile in return. "I have to check your back side."

"Backside? You must be kidding."

His face is red all over again. "I don't mean it like that. I just mean your back *half*. I just checked your front half."

"And you think my father put a chip up my ass?" I snort. "OSG are assholes, but they're not deviants."

"You sure about that? Because I've found chips in some very strange places, trust me. My scan isn't officially done until I scan you at one hundred percent. We're at sixty right now."

"Fine." I throw my arms up and turn around. "Scan my ass. See for yourself. I'm clean."

I roll my eyes to the ceiling as the wand is moving up my legs to the top of my butt, but just as I'm about to tell him to go screw himself and his damn wand, the fucking beeper starts sounding from inside his box.

"A-*ha!*" he yells, glee coloring his words. "Found ya!"

"You *bitch*," Lucinda says with way more venom than I deserve.

I spin around and grab at the box hanging around his neck. "Let me see that thing. You're lying. This is broken. That's a false reading."

His words come out strained as the tightened strap around his neck cuts off his airway. "No way, lady. This machine was calibrated today. It's in perfect condition. You have a chip in your lower back." He yanks it back from me and adjusts the strap so it's not choking him anymore.

"Like hell I do." I glare at him.

He reaches around behind me with the wand and it beeps again. He grins. "See? Second reading. Same as the first."

"Give me that." I yank the wand out of his hand and put it on him —nothing—, then on Lucinda's neck — nothing—, then on my lower back again. The machine beeps really loudly.

My breaths come out in ragged huffs, and my ears are burning with anger and embarrassment. I feel like I'm going to vomit right here on my own boots. *How can this be? How can I have a chip in me? Who put it there? Was it my father? Would he do that?* Surely I would have remembered something like that happening to me. Known about it. Had some sort of clue. *What in the hell is the chip even for? What's it doing to me? Is it used to control me? To keep track of me?* I'm getting sicker by the second.

"Don't worry," Jens says, very happy with himself. "I can get it out for you."

"She probably doesn't want it out," Lucinda says, sneering. "Then her team won't be able to find her later when they come to take over our ship."

I shove her out of the way so I'm not tempted to punch her in the face. "Take it out. Right now." I'm sweating with the sense of urgency that's overtaking my rational, thinking mind. If this thing is a tracker, I need to get it out of me and send it through a wormhole to another galaxy. My father cannot find me, no matter what. I know too much, I've seen too much, and I'm not going back there.

Jens hurries to take the machine from around his neck and puts it down with a clatter onto his workbench. "You'll have to come to our medical chamber. It could be in there pretty deep."

I'm standing in the middle of this kid's workstation wondering what the hell I should do next, and my ship is floating out there with only one person onboard who I can trust. All the other crew members would probably love nothing more than to get rid of me, and for all I know, my father could be coming for me right now. I've never felt so vulnerable in my entire life as I do right now. *What to do, what to do, what to do?*

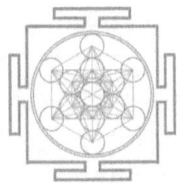

CHAPTER
TWENTY-TWO

AFTER CONFIRMING VIA COMM THAT Baebong is in control of my ship and Beltz is behaving himself onboard, I submit myself to the surgical interventions of a fifteen year old virgin. Obviously, I'm desperate and very possibly losing my mind.

"Now, don't move," he says. "You refused the anesthetic, so this is going to burn like nothing you've ever felt before."

"I doubt it," I say, a memory of my father roasting the skin of my arm with a dry-laser still quite clear in my mind and heart. It might have been a full five years ago, but it seems like it was just last week that I was moving through my eighth level of training. I passed my POW versions with flying colors, and I have the scars to show for it, having refused to allow my father to remove them with MI. I used to wear them to remind him of how far he was willing to go in the name of the OSG and his career. Now I wear them to remember, and to help me not to ever become complacent. The scars never bothered him as much as they bothered me, though.

The first slice into my back is clean, burning as promised, but I can take it. My grip on the bars below the medical table increases only slightly. Lying face down, my head turned to the side, I notice the inner-lit shelves across the chamber that house their medical supplies, all of which are lined up neatly and very possibly alphabetized. It makes me wonder if my ship is as prepared as this one is for medical emergencies. I should probably check that with Jeffers when I get back onboard.

The chip-tracking machine beeps again.

"Sorry," Jens says. "Just verifying I'm in the right place." He sounds very nervous. Maybe I should be too, but there's no space in my world for nerves right now. I need to focus. Focus on the pain and managing it.

Lucinda's expression catches my eye. Her skin has gone a little pale, and her gaze moves to the ceiling as the laser knife cuts deeper into my back.

My training kicks in without conscious effort on my part. One moment I'm feeling the fire of the cutter searing my skin, the next I'm seeing colors. The pain isn't real. It's merely a single color in the spectrum of many. *Orange.* I see orange and then yellow in place of the pain. I do not succumb to it. Allowing those negative sensations to enter my consciousness is weakness, and weakness is downfall. *Weakness is downfall. Weakness is downfall…*

Deep inside myself I turn, oblivious to what's happening around me, knowing only that I am here inside this room with two other people and they do not need my conscious thought with them right now.

Orange tries to fill my field of vision, but I control it. I force it down into a very small square, a size no bigger than the picochip in my back. And there I leave it; insignificant, helpless in the face of my power. A color cannot hurt me anymore than a spoken word can.

Pain can be mastered and controlled. I learned this from an early age. My training started with simple steps. First, to learn the difference between levels of pain. To appreciate them and understand how they work inside my brain and at the ends of my nerves. With help from a nerve control device and then later with mere mind control, I learned to shut off the parts of me that could feel, to numb their responses down to the point that even when my skin was being cut open, I would sense nothing more than a bit of pressure. I'm out of practice now, but in the prime of my training regimen, an enemy could have removed one of my eyeballs and I wouldn't even have winced.

"Hello? Hello? Are you in there?"

A beard-prickled face is looming before mine. First its outline is fuzzy, and then it slowly comes into focus. My nose scrunches up as my other senses return.

"Jesus, what'd you eat for lunch? Rotten chicken?" I push his face away from me, smooshing his nose sideways in the process.

Jens smiles as he stands. "No. Schwenkbraten. You can sit up now. We're all done here."

I do a push-up and then fling myself off the side of the table, landing on my feet with only a slight sway before I'm steady again. The lower half of my flight suit is undone, so I busy myself with buckling up as Jens cleans off the table I was just occupying.

When I look up, I find Lucinda staring at me.

"What?" I'm cranky, always a little out of sorts after withdrawing from pain like that. Coming back to reality is never my favorite thing. I used to think one day I'd stay inside my head forever and never come out. I tried it once; I lasted three days before my father had me nearly drowned to bring me back. Stupid survival instincts had my lungs burning, and then I had to return to reality. He was not happy with me that week and seemed to enjoy way too much expressing that feeling.

"He cut really deep into your back," Lucinda says, her voice wavering.

"So?" I look over at the tray that holds used, bloody soak pads and shiny, metal instruments stained red. The smell of cooked flesh lingers in the room. I'm happy to know the DS Mekanika has a suturing laser. Walking around with old-school threads in my skin is not my favorite thing in the universe. They tend to pull under my tight flight suit.

"*So*, it had to hurt."

"Not really. Nothing has to hurt if you don't let it. Pain is all in your head."

Jens is busy cleaning up. "She's been trained to manage her pain." He looks over at me and nods in appreciation. "I thought Jacov was good, but he's not as good as you. Very impressive."

I shrug. I paid a very high price for the ability to impress people like that. I wish I'd been given a choice in the matter, because I think I would have been happy using anesthetic like normal people.

"That can't be real," Lucinda says, taking a small step backward, flinching when she bangs into the surgery tray and makes all the instruments on top clatter.

"No, of course it can't," I say bitterly. She's right; for her it can't be real. She'd never understand the things I went through, the burdens people like my father insist others bear in the name of the OSG. "Come on, let's go."

"Where are you going?" Jens asks, stopping his work at the cleaning station to stare at me.

"Back to my ship."

"Don't you want to discuss this thing?" He points at the chip clipped with a set of tweezers he must have used to pull it out of my skin.

"What's to discuss? Some OSG asshole put a chip in me. You took it out. It won't work on me anymore, will it?"

"No. It works with biorhythms. I don't have all the details yet about how it works or what its purpose is, but I'm working on it."

"Incinerate it for me, would you?"

"Actually, I'm planning to reverse engineer it."

I stride over before he has a chance to react and snatch it up. "Like hell you are." I yank the clamps off it and throw the empty tool toward the tray. It clatters against the metal and falls to the floor.

"Hey!" he shouts at my back, but I'm already headed out the door, my fist closed around that stupid chip tight enough to press its imprint into my palm.

"Wait for me!" Lucinda shouts, squeezing through the opening to the door that's quickly getting smaller. She's barely through before it's closed. Jens's voice comes through it muffled.

"You can't get off the ship without Jacov escorting you!"

"Escort my ass." I walk at a fast clip down the corridor while I try to orient myself. I hesitate at the fork in the path before me. *Am I supposed to go left here or right?*

Lucinda grabs my arm. "This way." She yanks me to the left, and I have to take a few stumbling steps sideways before I'm upright again.

Lifting my hand to my mouth, I simultaneously bend my thumb in toward my palm to activate the commset attached to my wrist. The small device I strapped on before we left the Anarchy is live, thank goodness; its green light glows in my hand. "We're on our way back. Are the doors open?"

There's a three-second pause before Baebong's voice comes over the frequency. "Yes, but there's a giant mountain of a guy at your end, and he doesn't look very friendly."

"Jacov." I hiss out an annoyed breath. "Dammit."

"Leave him to me," Lucinda says, walking faster as she reaches into one of the pockets of her white coat. Its sides flap against her legs, and the back flies up as her speed continues to increase. I'm almost to the point of jogging to keep up with her when she suddenly comes up short.

"Wait," she says. "We need that boom chuck, right? We shouldn't leave without it."

"We still have Beltz on the Anarchy. If we have to, we'll trade him and the nuts for it."

She grins, but it doesn't look like a happy expression. "Fine."

We walk side by side, down the corridor that will take us to the airlock connecting our ships, the bottoms of our boots clanking against the metal grating below. We sound like we're going into battle, and I'm not so sure that we're not.

CHAPTER TWENTY-THREE

JACOV IS WAITING THERE FOR us, and I open my mouth to tell him we're leaving, but Lucinda gets there before me.

"Step out of the way. We're leaving your ship." Her arms are clenched at her sides.

"No one leaves."

"I do." She puts her hand into her coat pocket and lifts something out, aiming it at his face. A hiss comes from whatever is in her hand, and a small cloud of something vaporized hits him in the eyes.

He blinks several times as tears well up.

She hisses her can of stuff at him a second time.

He reaches up and yanks it out of her hand.

"What the hell?" she asks. "That's pure capsaicin!"

Jacov's eyes are blood red at this point, but he hasn't

moved other than to look at what he took from her and then throw it over his shoulder. The tiny canister clanks against the wall and then falls to the grated metal floor, rolling a few centimeters before it comes to a stop against his boot.

Lucinda takes two steps back until she's even with me. "He should be screaming in pain right now." She glances at me. "What's wrong with you people, anyway?"

Ignoring her insult, I tilt my head as I look at Jacov more closely. Then I smile when I notice what he's doing. His thumb is very gently tapping each of his other fingers of the same hand in turn. Over and over, he touches them as he maintains control over the pain. I'd recognize that technique anywhere. I used it myself when I was in Level 2 training.

"I guess I'm not the only OSG reject aboard the DS Mekanika, am I?"

Jacov's jaw muscles clench up but he doesn't say a word.

Lucinda throws her arms up. "Great. We're screwed."

I shake my head. "I don't think so." Taking three steps toward Jacov, I stop just in front of him, looking up so I can meet his eyes. "I need to get back on my ship, trade your captain for that part, and deliver him back to you. We have no fight with you." My hand rests on my knife very casually. It's not necessarily a threat, but I see him glance down at it and readjust his stance in response. We speak the same language, and I know he doesn't want to mess with me.

He stares down at me, tears breaking free to roll down his cheeks as he suffers the physical effects of the oil sprayed into them. It gives me the strangest impression of him crying over the fact that I want to leave. Flashbacks come to me of the day I disappeared from my father's station. He never cried a single tear for me, I'm sure of that, even though I didn't actually see him the day I left. I was in such a hurry to leave, I jumped on a garbage scow and never looked back. That chip in my back was just another means to control me. What I can't figure out, and I'm going to have to mull it over later, is why my father never sought to use it to find me, because the thing was obviously live. *Maybe it's not used for tracking.* Just the thought sends a shiver down my spine.

Jacov blinks three times before responding. "You need a dead chicken."

I wasn't expecting that. "What?"

"What is going on with the dead chickens?" Lucinda asks, frustrated. "It's a health hazard, not to mention disgusting."

His gaze never leaves me as he answers her. "Decomposition masks the signal from the revelation disk."

"Revelation disk?" Now I'm not as focused on getting off his ship as I am on knowing what he's talking about. Obviously he means the disk we found in our incinerator, but how does decomposition affect it? *Why does it even exist? And what exactly does it do besides make a person pass out?*

A voice comes over the comm next to the airlock.

"Jacov? Status." It's Beltz.

I speak up before Jacov can answer. "Status is I'm ready to come back to my ship. Let's do this trade so we can get our water."

Beltz says something to Jacov in a language I don't know, and Jacov responds in kind, his eyes remaining on me.

"Very interesting," Beltz says. I can hear a smile in his voice. "Okay, we are ready to make a trade. You come back."

I raise an eyebrow at Jacov, and he slowly moves out of my way. Lucinda and I waste no time walking through the first airlock, her behind me. She catches up and draws even with me shoulder to shoulder so she can whisper in my ear. Her hot breath makes me want to shove her away, but I resist. She doesn't need any more reasons to dislike me.

"What's going on? Where are we going after this? What's your plan?"

"Why?" I ask, hesitating at the entrance to the Anarchy. "I thought you were planning on hitching a ride with Beltz."

Her chin goes up. "No. I never said that. And I have a right to know where the ship I'm living on is going."

"We'll talk later." With that, I step through the airlock and onto the Anarchy. Everyone is waiting there for me, including Baebong. He doesn't look happy.

CHAPTER
TWENTY-FOUR

MY SHIP LOOKS DIFFERENT TO me. I don't know if it's the glares I'm getting from the crew or the dirt-encrusted corners I see everywhere now that I've been onboard a clean DS. Either way, I'm not going to stand for it. I didn't risk being Langlade's concubine to be downgraded to asshole of the century on my own ship.

"Let's get this done," I say to Beltz.

"Before we do that, I'd like to know what's going on with that chip or whatever," Baebong says, trying to sound tough. His shoulders go back and his chest puffs out, as if that's going to intimidate me into following his orders.

I stop right in front of him, barely hanging onto my shit. "The day you decide what happens on my ship is the day I'm floating and my blood is crystallizing in my exploding veins. You're not the captain here, I am. You don't like it? You're welcome to leave." I gesture behind me. "There's the door."

He blinks a few times, expressionless.

I shift my glare to the gingers. "You have something you want to say?"

Tam shakes his head side to side with vigor.

"No, Ma'am," Gus says, "not us. We're just the engineers. We live to serve."

Tam elbows his brother in the ribs, but says nothing to contradict his statement.

"Good." I push past them, not waiting to hear Jeffers' or Rollo's opinions. Jeffers' penetrating stare is enough to get me saying something I'll probably regret, and since I can't yet read him, I'm not going to assume what he's thinking is as bad as what Baebong obviously is. "Let's get up on the flightdeck. I don't like being this close to the OSG without eyes-on." I need to see for myself that they're nowhere around before I can settle down and think straight to come up with a plan. Right now my brain is screaming only one thing: *Get away!* But I'm not sure that's the best course of action yet. I need more information about this disk and the chip that's in my breast pocket.

"You want me to arrange for the transport of the boom chuck?" Beltz asks.

"No. I'd like you to follow me so we can discuss this disk."

"The disk you don't have, you mean?" he asks, laughter in his tone.

"Exactly." I'm around the corner of the corridor before I realize Lucinda's keeping up with me.

"What do you want?" I practically growl.

She talks in a hurried whisper. "I just wanted to tell you that I'm on your side."

A bitter laugh escapes me. "Oh yeah? Sure. For now you are."

"Beggars can't be choosy."

I stop so quickly, she bumps into me. "I've never been a beggar in my life. You can go if you don't like it here. It means nothing to me." That's not exactly the truth, but I don't like being called a beggar.

We stare each other down, and I watch as several emotions buzz past her face. The first one has me almost scratching my head. *Hurt?* Then I see frustration, anger, and finally, resignation.

"I like it here just fine." Her chin goes up a notch. "If I can live with Langlade, living with you will be nothing in comparison."

I smile, kind of evil-like. "We'll see about that." I'm not making anyone any promises. Living on my ship is not going to be like being at a station where everything is taken care of and you just have to show up. Shit is going to change around here, starting now.

The rest of the group is directly behind us at this point, so I continue on, stopping only to open the portal leading to the flightdeck. Taking my seat in the captain's chair, I turn to face the small crowd below me at the bottom of the stairs. I know this is a pivotal point in our relationship, but I'm too upset to think rationally and calmly. Instinct takes over my mouth and starts running the show.

"For those of you who don't already know, I had a picochip in my back that Beltz's cousin Jens removed." I shift my focus to Beltz. "What was it?"

He shrugs. "Maybe a locator. Maybe something else. We won't know until my cousin reverse-engineers it."

I shake my head. "Sorry, but he's not going to be doing that." I resist the urge to pat my pocket where I've stashed the chip. I have plans for this little bastard, and it doesn't include the thing remaining in existence. "Tell me about the disk."

"Ah, the disk." Beltz looks down at the ground and shakes his head. "That information is for people who need to know."

The words come out as a growl because I'm almost out of patience. "Trust me; I need to know."

He shrugs and smiles at me. "Only those in the Alliance need to know. You are not in the Alliance."

"What alliance?" I narrow my eyes at him, wondering if he's blowing ice crystals up my butt.

"Again, I will say, if you do not have the disk, I cannot help you."

"You wanted to take that disk from us," Baebong says, stepping forward, walking up the first stair up to the flightdeck before he turns back around.

My heart warms when I realize he's aligning himself with me against the rest of the group. Unconscious or not, I know his move means he's still with me. Thank the universe for that, because I really don't want to be on the opposite end of one of his ridiculous weapons. They have a tendency to vaporize things.

Beltz shrugs again. "Ships that are not a part of the Alliance have no need for the disk."

I sigh heavily, tired of the subject already. "Listen, Beltz, we have a disk, but it's not for sale. I want to know about this Alliance and who's a part of it and what your next move is."

"But you had a chip in your back. You are OSG. Or you *were*, at least."

"I was a kid born into an OSG family. That doesn't make me OSG. And your buddy Jacov was OSG too, so don't act like you discriminate all that much."

Beltz thinks he's as smooth as ice, but I see the flicker of curiosity in his eyes. "I am surprised he told you."

"He didn't have to."

"So." Beltz is done messing around. Standing up straight, he delivers his next words with conviction. "You are a little girl who had a picochip in her back and you need a boom chuck. I am a man of simple means. I want the disk. We can make a trade."

I shake my head. "No deal. You already struck the terms, and you can't change them now."

"But you told me you did not have the disk. You lied. That is not nice to lie to me." His threat is unmistakable.

"Nothing in the books or our customs says I need to tell you what my ship's inventory is. That disk is inventory as far as I'm concerned. You agreed to trade one Mekanika Special Boom Chuck for nuts, and that's the trade that's going to happen."

Rollo's head starts bobbing from the back of the group and he gives me a thumbs up along with a wink. I have to battle not to roll my eyes and sigh at his obvious and goofy approval. But at least I know I got it right in his world; and according to Baebong, his world is all about finding hard to find things.

"And if I refuse?" Beltz straightens to his full height, which is impressive, but not as intimidating as he thinks it is. Not to me, anyway. Lucinda and Rollo look like they want to run, though.

I shrug. "Then I'll board your ship with weaponry, take it, and leave you with nothing."

"No nuts," Rollo adds, putting on a show of bravery I know he doesn't really feel. He holds up two fingers bent over. "That's how it works. You snake on a deal, you get fanged."

Everyone turns to look at him.

"What?" He shrugs. "Rollo knows the traders' code. It's a rule. You can look it up."

Beltz stares at me for the longest time. The flightdeck goes silent, save for a couple boot shuffles and throat clearings. Then footsteps take up all the sound space as Baebong mounts the rest of the steps and claims his seat as my navigator.

Jeffers is next. He takes the seat behind me and to my right. That's three people I can count on now. *Booyah*.

"If you need me, I'll be in my work chamber," Lucinda says.

I nod at her, grateful for her foresight. Had she said she was going to the biogrid, it would have clued Beltz in to what else we've hidden from him on our ship. As far as he's concerned, she's just a regular old grower, not a biogrid genius. Yes, I called her a genius. I'm feeling pretty generous right now. And why wouldn't I be? I have a crew again. *Hell yeah!*

Gus lifts a finger. "We have some things to do in the engine room, soo…later, humans." He and Tam disappear behind a swoosh of the portal door.

Rollo walks around to stand next to Beltz, facing him. "Are we doing this deal or not? Clock's ticking. Better decide soon or the rate goes up."

Beltz looks slowly over at him, but Rollo doesn't move. I say nothing, waiting for things to play out.

"You look like you could use a nice blue ring around your eye," Beltz says to him.

Rollo frowns. "And you look like someone who could use a reminder about what happens to people who back out of negotiated deals." He looks over at me. "You want me to get the float-lock ready?"

I nod.

Rollo leaves out the flightdeck door, probably to go hide somewhere, seeing as how he has no idea where the float chamber is, and I'm pretty sure his bluster is just that. But he did do a good job of reminding Beltz about trader conventions. Hopefully it'll make him think twice before he puts his finger on a trigger.

Beltz looks at me and waits.

"You have the deal in front of you," I say, calm as hell. "Make your decision." My heart is hammering away, but he'll never know. My training allows me to keep my exterior calm while my insides flip and twist in on themselves.

His bottom lip comes out and then he nods, very slowly. "I have made my decision."

I raise my eyebrows. "And?"

"I decide that maybe you want to know about the Alliance."

"Insightful." Or not, since I already asked about it. I have to be patient and let him work his way through this, though. I have a feeling this Alliance thing might be something we could use to our advantage, if having disks that can activate in the presence of picochips is part of the deal.

"We must discuss it in private," he says. "Captain to captain. No crew."

"Fine." I look to my left and right. Baebong and Jeffers take the hint and leave through the portal that leads to Lucinda's chamber. I suspect, however, that Baebong will wait just outside the door. This fact allows me to be more confident while alone on the flightdeck with this hulking form of a man who I'm still not sure I can trust.

Beltz rocks up on his toes and then back to his heels, his hands clasped behind him. "So, you are former OSG. Tell me about that."

I tap a finger on the arm of my chair. "Tell me about the Alliance."

"We will trade information." He smiles. "You first."

I weigh the risk of sharing a little of my history against learning about this so-called Alliance, and decide I can part with some of the basics. He already knows about the picochip.

"My father is an OSG commander. I was born into it. I was trained until I was sixteen as part of the Defense Squadron before I left."

"What level of training did you reach?"

I shake my head. "Nope. It's your turn now. Tell me about the Alliance."

He shrugs. "We are a group of drifters who seek to work together to combat the growing influence of the OSG on our operations. Now you."

"I reached Level Ten."

He frowns. "That cannot be true."

"Sure it can."

"No one reaches Level Ten at your age. I know men in their thirties who have not yet reached it."

"Jacov for example?" I wait for him to deny it, but he says nothing. "Your turn. I answered your question, now you answer mine: who's part of the Alliance?"

"I cannot reveal ship or captain identifiers, but I can tell you that it is all drifters. We do not accept government-tainted members."

That leaves out cargo ships, transporters, and pretty much every other class of ship in the universe. *Interesting.*

"How many of you are there?"

He shakes his head. "It's your turn. Show me your Level Ten."

I lift an eyebrow. "You want me to slit your throat?" I still remember my final training: a fight to the death. I stopped just before the guy's artery was laid open, but not before I'd sent my opponent into a very deep sleep that probably took months to wake from. I didn't stick around long enough after that fight to find out the details.

"I prefer to see other evidence."

I sigh as I push up my sleeve. "POW training. Level Nine. That's the best I can do without hurting someone."

He steps forward and examines my scars more closely, grunting and nodding when he sees the extent of it. "You did not use MI. Why?"

I smile. "My turn. How many are in the Alliance?"

"We are four at this time."

"Four including Langlade? That makes you three. Regardless, that's not going to make any difference if the OSG decides it's going to bend you over."

He looks at me for the first time with a very serious expression. There's no humor there, no threat, no nothing except maybe a promise. "You would be surprised what four like-minded groups of people can accomplish."

His answer makes me even more curious, as does the fact that he failed to answer the part about Langlade. I'm not much of a group activities person, but the idea of four other DSs having my back is definitely appealing.

"The MI," he prompts. "Why not?" He points at my arm.

I push my sleeve back down. "So I won't forget."

"So *you* won't forget or so the person who did it won't forget?"

I stare at him, wondering if he's that uber perceptive or just shooting into the Dark.

"Makes no difference either way, does it?" I stand and walk down the stairs to be at his level, which forces me to have to look up to meet his eyes. "The OSG is trying to tax our water, but you knew that already. Looks like you've known about it for a while, and you're preparing yourself for some kind of conflict with that cloaking system you have. What else do they have planned? Do you know? Where are you getting your information?"

"Do *you* know what they have planned?" He's challenging me. This, I know; but what I don't know is how to respond. Now I'm the one shooting into the Dark.

It's his turn to respond to my questions, but I'm willing to invest a little more of myself to get some better answers. "I know that until now, the OSG has been focused on settlements and putting together their infrastructures. They say their sole mission is to populate any habitable planetary surface with our species, but I always wondered why they spent so much time training us how to kill each other when they claimed to want a peaceful existence."

"A very astute observation. Shall I tell you about realpolitik, the true version of the OSG's plan for our universe?"

His words make me want to run out of the room behind Lucinda and Rollo, or hide in the engine room with Gus and Tam. But I'm the captain of this ship now, so I don't have the luxury of being a coward. Half of me is sad about that and the other half is ready to go kick some OSG ass.

"By all means." I fold my arms over my chest, waiting to hear his theory, hoping it won't dredge up any memories I'd rather keep suppressed.

CHAPTER
TWENTY-FIVE

BELTZ LOWERS HIMSELF TO A step, sitting on it as he rests his elbows on his bent knees. I take the step nearby, turning to slightly face him. My arms remain folded, although now raised to my knees as well. It's weird that I feel a kinship with him, but maybe it shouldn't be; we're both captains, we both don't trust the OSG, and we both think it's funny when someone gets the better of us and cuts us open for it.

"I do not know who your father is, but if he is part of the OSG, and he recruited his own daughter to their fighting forces, then of course I am speaking to someone who has heard, first hand, of their realpolitik." A special kind of furor overtakes Beltz's words and makes me want to lean in to hear them more clearly. "They say to the universe that they want peace and diplomacy, but believe me, when that fails, they are not afraid to use the big stick."

"The big stick?"

He waves my comment off. "Oh, do not worry. It is just a very old maxim in the government. They used to say when our ancestors walked the Earth that a strong leader must speak softly and carry a big stick." He points at me. "When you were with your father, you were part of that big stick. You and many like you are part of their threat. And their particle weapons of course, they are a part of the big stick. The drifters do not have a chance against something like that." He scowls. "I do not care what they say to you and to me. The OSG is not about peace and nice, pretty little biodomes on the planets for all the families. It is about dominance and submission. You guess who is to submit." He nods once to let me know it's us, as if I didn't already know that.

"So what's the point of the Alliance?" I ask. "What's your mission?"

"As one single drifter, we are doomed to subservience and slavery. To eventual grounding. We are much easier to control on the ground, are we not? But as a group, we are not doomed. At least we have a chance."

"A chance to what? Defeat the OSG?" Disbelief colors my tone. He must be insane if he thinks four drifters could even punch a hole in the OSG.

"No, not to defeat anyone. To *live*. To remain independent and free to make our own choices." He leans in closer. "That is all we want to do. To live our lives the way we want, without some big brother telling us what we must and must not do."

I nod. I get where he's coming from completely. "So this Alliance is not for fighting against the OSG?"

His tone lightens. "Oh, sure, we can fight if we must. But more so, we can communicate. We can trade. We can be eyes in four places, not just one." He leans in closer and whispers. "Five, if you join us." He winks.

"And those five *do* or *don't* include Langlade?" After taking his ship, I'm kind of in the mood to avoid him for the next fifty years or so.

His expression goes dark. "No, it does not."

"Then why does he have a disk?"

"Forget Langlade. Do you see the value of the Alliance, or are you so much of an anarchist that you cannot imagine yourself working with others toward a common goal?"

I shake my head, seeing the need for it and the benefits. Everything he's said about the OSG rings true against the things I already know and have seen and heard growing up in my father's household.

"It's not that I'm an anarchist, but any alliance like you're talking about depends completely on trust." I say this to him knowing that this particular resource is in short supply throughout the Dark. Even Baebong kind of let me down today, getting all suspicious on me. To be fair, though, I never did trust him enough to tell him my family history. It makes me sad to think that in my search for independence, I've managed so well to find loneliness. I'm only now realizing how different the two concepts are.

"That is right. Trust is imperative. And so we have the disk. That is part of it. The other part...," he shrugs, "... well, that is just faith. We have faith in each other, faith that we have the same goals and realize that we're better off together than apart. United, we stand. Divided, we fall. Another maxim from long ago."

I laugh a little to myself as I realize my childish notions of being a drifter are just that: silly dreams of a young girl. "So being a drifter isn't about being alone and self-reliant?"

"It is, to some degree. But again, not really. No one can be truly alone for a long time. We are humans, after all. We crave the company of others. It is in our blood, our instinct. It is what keeps our race free from defects and strange happenings. We must keep the gene pool deep, eh?" He reaches over and nudges me, sending a jolt of something electric up my arm and into my chest. His arm is warm.

I glare at him. "What did I tell you about touching me without my permission?"

He smiles back. "What can I say? I have a very small memory for nonsense like that."

"We'll see if you still consider it nonsense when I stick you in the jewels with my knife," I mutter. Then in a louder voice, I ask, "What's the deal with the disk and the chicken?"

"I can only tell you if you are in the Alliance." He shrugs, but smiles.

It's almost charming when he looks at me like that. *Is he flirting with me? Yikes.* He's out of my league. I can tell from the look of him that he's had a lot of women in his bunk.

"Are you inviting me in?" I ask, hoping I don't sound like I'm flirting back.

"I don't know," he says slyly. "Can I trust you?"

I stare him down. "Can I trust *you*?"

I can't help thinking about my father and how easily he sold me out for his cause — for his realpolitik or whatever Beltz called it. He should have been someone I trusted with my life, but I could always trust my father to treat me like he treated all his other troops: as someone expendable, someone to be used for his own purposes

— purposes he didn't share with those who didn't have a need to know. I've been a pawn before, and I'll never allow myself to be one again.

But Beltz is right about one thing; we can't survive out here alone as a single drifter ship if the OSG is planning on making a move toward controlling our resources — especially if that resource is water. We can trade for almost anything else, but water is something we need to have direct access to.

So far, the crew of the DS Mekanika says they can make that happen with their boom chuck. And that locator device Jens used on me worked really well at finding that picochip. With a fabrication ship like Beltz's on my side, I could get the DS Anarchy in tiptop shape in no time. The idea of allying myself with them is positively energizing, but only *if* I can trust this Captain Gunter Beltz. That's a big *if* in my world.

I study Beltz's face, using my training to try and suss out any signs of deceit in his micro-expressions. All I see there is a frank openness and maybe a little heat. He keeps flicking glances at my chest.

He shrugs. "Trust for me is easy. I see you, I like you, I believe you, I trust you. If you double cross me, I kill you. End of the story."

I can live with that; at least he's honest. "Same goes for me."

He holds out his hand. "We bind our promise by the hand."

I look at the paw that's twice the size of mine, wondering if I'm going to regret taking it.

"Go ahead, Crazy Bitch, I am not going to hurt you."

My smile is slow in coming, but then it finally breaks out as I realize I'd rather have this guy on my side than against it.

"Call me crazy bitch one more time, and I'm going to have to cut you."

His head falls back as he barks out a huge laugh, his hand enveloping mine in warmth. Another sizzle of electric heat moves through me, this time not nearly as unwelcome as it was before.

CHAPTER
TWENTY-SIX

STANDING IN THE ENGINE ROOM next to Baebong, I reflect on my first twenty-four hours as Captain of the DS Anarchy. *Is this even real? Did I actually win this ship in a card game and then drive it straight into a political astroid storm of epic proportions necessitating the joining of a rebel alliance?* Either I'm dreaming while suffering under the influence of some serious chemicals or my life has gone completely out of the galaxy. I don't know which to hope is true.

The twins are busy installing the new boom chuck with Adelle's help, and Jeffers is making a meal. I've lost track of which meal it is. *Lunch? Dinner?* I told him not to make anything too fancy. I'm still not ready to reveal to Beltz and his crew the extent of our biogrid, even though we're now an unofficial part of his Alliance —hoping to be made official upon a voting of the rest of the Alliance members— and his crew is coming to join us at the table. Our first meeting with the entire Alliance group is scheduled to take place ten hours after Tam is telling me our ice-grab will be completed. I'm trying to talk myself out of being nervous, but it's not working.

"We're all set down here," Gus says, speaking from inside the boom cab below the ship. The small clearpanel there allows him to watch as one of Adelle's robotic systems attaches the boom chuck on the mechanism that will soon be lowered to a position outside of the hull. Like most people I've known, Tam and Gus avoid doing any Dark-walking, and I support that. I've seen too many people unintentionally float when something's gone wrong. Adelle's here for a purpose, and I intend to find out all she's capable of; after which, I'll exploit her systems as much and as often as is reasonable, safe, and smart. So far, I'm impressed. Apparently, Gus and Tam have given her a few upgrades, which is pretty amazing considering the budget they've had to work with.

"Good," I say. "When will you be ready to start the process?"

"Fifteen minutes."

Tam leans in and whispers in my ear. "More like twenty."

"Good." I nod at Tam. "I'll be on the flightdeck waiting for your go signal. How close do I need to be to the surface?"

"Two thousand meters?" Gus says it like he's afraid to even hear it coming out of his own mouth.

I can't control the hiss that comes with my sharp intake of breath. *Two thousand meters? Is he insane?*

"It's the only way we can do it and not be detected," Tam says, sounding like he's apologizing. "I talked with that Jens kid. It's how they do it on the Mekanika."

I shrug, acting like it's not the huge, death-defying maneuver that it is. *If Beltz can do it, I can too, right?* "Yeah, I get it. Just give me a shout when you're ready."

I leave the engine room and stride down the corridor, talking to myself the whole way. *You can do this. You've done it a hundred times on the simulator. Even closer ice-grabs than this. And you have Adelle. She can smooth out your approach. The systems are good. The ship is in decent shape. And after it's all over, we'll be meeting our new allies. Don't freak out. Don't freak out. You can do this.* My flightsuit is sticking to me with sweat. Again.

The portal to the flightdeck is before me. I stare at it for a few seconds before waving my hand over the keypad. Beyond this door lies the controls I must take in hand and use to maneuver this ship into grabbing ice directly from the surface of Xylera from a mere two thousand meters above, while walls of ice and who the hell knows what else surge up from the surface and threaten to swallow my ship whole. *I must be insane.*

I let out the breath I was holding and walk through the portal. If I'm going to die, at least it'll be a quick death. The ice of Xylera freezes solid anything that gets within eight hundred meters of it, including drifter ships and the people who crew them.

CHAPTER
TWENTY-SEVEN

BACK ON THE FLIGHTDECK AFTER my little mission to stash the picochip in the delivery chute of the water uptake boom, I find Beltz waiting for me. He pledged to guide me through my first ice-grab, even though I told him I didn't need his help loud enough for everyone to hear me. Inside, though, I'm glad for his presence, and I think he knows it. It makes me wonder if he had a mentor when he started.

As I take my seat, he stands behind me, silent but for the occasional grunt or hiss of breath as I begin our descent toward Xylera's surface. We're still in clear view of anyone looking our way, but without our boom out, we look like anyone else just settling into a planet's atmosphere for a little bit of time away from the dangers of flying space junk and random asteroids. We won't be swallowed by Xylera's famous mists for another few thousand meters.

I slowly guide the DS Anarchy closer to the surface of the ice planet, mindful of the weather systems circulation map that's being displayed on one of the clearpanels ahead of me and to the left. *So far so good.* There are no storms that I can see anywhere close by, and we have only another four or five thousand meters to go. I've only been sitting here for ten minutes, but it feels like an hour.

"Easy does it," says Baebong, his fingers flying over the navigation array as he communicates with Adelle's systems. "Easy… We're at six point eight thousand meters and dropping ten meters per second. We don't need to get there yesterday."

"You must like hanging around here or something," I say flippantly. I moved twice this fast in the simulator when I practiced my ice-grabs. But then again, that simulator never creaked and groaned the way the DS Anarchy is doing right now. *Is that normal? Was the simulator I used missing a sound effect module?*

"Ship surface integrity check," I say to Jeffers, not sure if he'll know what I mean if I use the acronym we learned in the sim. S-S-I means nothing if you don't have the training.

He sounds nervous when he answers me. "The computer says eighty percent fore, ninety-three aft, sixty-eight below deck, Captain."

"That's not good," I mumble to myself. I'm even more motivated to go quickly now. I can't have parts of the ship sloughing off before we're finished. Xylera's gravitational force will swallow them up, and we'll have to do without, and those parts are expensive, not to mention sometimes absolutely necessary for continued safe flight and landing.

"Three thousand meters, descending two hundred meters per second."

"Not too fast, Captain," Beltz says from behind me. "You will get there. Be patient."

"That's easy for you to say." I glare at the clearpanel before me that shows what's going on below the ship. The white and blue colors of Xylera ice are taking up the entire frame now. No longer is the Dark anywhere viewable below us. We're nearly to our final altitude when a change in the surface tension of the ice planet catches my eye.

"That doesn't look good," I mumble mostly to myself. I've heard about ships getting hit with a huge wave and being dragged down into the ice never to be seen again, and I don't want that to be our fate. The gravitational field coming from Xylera is pulling at the ship, but Adelle counteracts it with the thrust I've programmed at my array, lightening the gravitational field on the ship to ensure we can still move about freely. But if an ice wave hits us, it'll throw everything off.

"I'm getting an alert over here," Jeffers says.

"Talk to me," I say, all my attention on my own business. A red flashing light tries to distract me off to my left, but I ignore it in favor of reading my boom readiness. The new chuck seems to be working just fine so far, which is good because without it, we might as well be a giant yo-yo on a string being flung around the planet by the boom not tethered to the ship properly.

I press the button that will release the first segment of the boom from its inner chamber. Exhaust vents open on either side of it automatically. The reverse pressure they provide will make it easier to grab that ice and water in one giant flow.

Jeffers' voice is shaking when he speaks again. "Ship surface integrity below deck is dropping rapidly. We're at forty-nine percent."

I swallow the lump in my throat. *Time to rock and roll.* "Commencing ice grab in *five*."

I flip the switch that floats up out of the array at my left hand. With my right, I use the joystick that controls the boom.

"We're not at altitude yet," Baebong says.

"*Four*... Too bad. If the OSG ship sees us, they see us. I can't risk the integrity of the ship." The mist from the planet's atmosphere won't cover us completely here, but I have to count on the fact that what I'm doing is so crazy, they won't think to be watching for it.

I feel a hand on my shoulder. "You're doing the right thing. Just keep going."

I shrug off Beltz's pat on the back, but it gives me the strength I need to continue and not cry my eyes out.

"*Three*," I say, continuing the countdown and flipping the lever that will lock the boom into place so it can begin its final descent. *Please don't let me destroy my ship!*

"Integrity dropping again," Jeffers says, louder this time. I'm not even sure he realizes he sounds like an old woman at this point. "Thirty-three!"

"*Two*... Holding here." I stop our descent and ready the ship for the uptake, the below deck thrusters set at forty-two percent burn to keep us from losing more altitude. Flipping the all-comm switch above me, I speak while still keeping my attention on my clearpanels. That fucking dark blue ice wave is coming closer, and I don't like the look of it one bit.

"Commencing ice-grab. All hands on deck." Things can get a little bumpy from here. I hope my crew knows that because it's too late for me to educate them.

Beltz flicks the all-comm off for me.

"*One*! Aaand we're launching the boom."

I punch in the numbers that I previously designated as the combination that would begin the sequence. A rumbling below deck is followed by a bunch of mechanical clanking sounds. Everyone's eyes are glued to the panel that shows the boom extending itself to maximum length, headed for the surface of Xylera. It doesn't have to go far, the pressure enough to pull the ice and water up to us. I can't help but think how phallic the damn thing is. I don't dare look at Baebong right now. He might make me laugh, and if that were to happen, I would sound unhinged. I'm that close to the edge of sanity right now.

"Below deck's structural integrity at twenty-nine percent now." Jeffers stands and turns to face me. "We should go. We're too close."

"No." I shake my head as sweat pours down my face from my temples. "We need the water." *And I need to get rid of this fucking picochip once and for all.* I surreptitiously punch in the code that will open the delivery chute's access door and let it fly out into the atmosphere of Xylera. A confirmation light flashing five seconds later tells me my secret mission was a success; the chute is empty of all foreign matter. *Find me now, Asshole. I'm swimming in the Sea of Xylera as far as you're concerned.*

The suction through the boom starts, and I keep my eye on the indicator that will show me how much ice and water we're taking on. It feels like we've been here for minutes already, but my timer says only twenty-three seconds have passed. We don't have nearly enough water to leave yet.

"Adelle!" I say much too loudly. *Dammit. Now they know I'm panicking.*

"Yes, Captain." Her computerized voice is calm and soothing. I'm glad Langlade picked her to be the compubot's host and not one of the other more commanding modules used to synthesize human speech. I really feel like I need a momma right now, and Adelle is fitting the bill. It makes me wonder why Langlade picked her. *Was he ever unsure about what he was doing on this ship?* I find it hard to believe that he was.

"What's going on with our integrity?" I ask, swiping with the back of my hand at a droplet of sweat that's tickling the edge of my ear.

"Failure to perform regular maintenance has compromised the integrity of the connections and seams below deck. I recommend a complete rehabilitation of the hull at your earliest convenience."

"When was the first time you noticed this little problem?" I ask angrily, my eyes glued to the water-level indicator readout. We're at a quarter of a megaliter. *Not enough.* And that ice wave is less than one klick from the bow of my ship. *Dammit!*

"One year ago," Adelle says, like she's *not* delivering the most shit-awful news I've ever heard in my life. "I reminded the former captain once per month at his request."

Rather than scream like a wild, unchained she-monster, I growl instead. "Bastard!" Langlade gave me a ship that he knew full well was in sore need of maintenance and didn't say a damn word about it. He was probably laughing as I walked away from that givit table. I guess the rumor that he spends a lot of credits keeping his fleet maintained in top shape was one of those myths that surrounded him.

"We have to go, Cass," Baebong says, sounding almost like he's going to cry. "The ship's going to break apart. I'm too young to die."

"Shut up, we're going to be fine. Stop being so dramatic. None of us are going to die until I say so." *Forty percent uptake. Come on, you fucking boom. Get me to eighty and I'll leave!* I can almost imagine the warm shower I'm going to have as soon as this is over. Maybe there'll be enough water to wash away the gallons of sweat I've accumulated in my clothing too. I can't remember the last time I had a proper washing. Most of my bathing over the past three years has been at a public sink.

The ship groans even louder. Then it begins to shake. I have to hang onto the arms of my chair to keep from sliding around in the big seat below my butt. *Sixty-two percent uptake. Come on, you bitch! Do this for me!*

"Time to leave," Beltz says.

"Eight more percent." My new goal drops from eighty percent to seventy. I can live with seventy percent. I'm determined to see this through. "We can do this." I shift my focus to my array, punching up a command for my onboard computer hostess with the mostest. "Adelle, get me a shield on that below deck area. Pick and choose, the weakest areas get the most shield. Go!"

"Yes, Captain. Partitioning shield on below-deck panels eight, nineteen, twenty-three…" Her voice keeps droning on with more panel numbers, but then a twin gets on the line and cuts her out.

"Hey! What's going on up there?! We're losing shield integrity all over the place!"

"I moved it to the below-deck area. I just need thirty more seconds." My voice is surprisingly calm, considering that inside I'm falling apart worse than my ship is.

"You have about five seconds and then we're going to bend over and kiss our own asses goodbye down here in the engine room."

"Copy that," I say, cutting off the comm.

Red lights flash on my array and on the clearpanel. The word ALERT in red floats as a hologram in the air in front of me. I've seen this in the simulator a few times, and I know it for the doom that it signals: I've hit the maximum stress level this ship can take. The next message I'm going to get is *Game Over* if I don't get the hell out of here.

Another blue alert shares the red one's screen space announcing the arrival of an ice wave big enough to eat my ship whole.

My fingers fly over the controls, cutting off the magnetic suction that was pulling the ice up, starting the retrieval sequence for the boom. "Hang on!" I yell as the farthest tip of the nearest ice wave hits the starboard side of the ship. I swear I can hear the crackling of the steeloid as it freezes on contact.

"Release the boom chuck!" I yell at Baebong, hoping none of that ice hit the boom at the point where it connects to the ship. Otherwise, my little maneuver isn't going to work; it'll just tear the boom free completely.

"We can't release yet! We'll lose it!"

"Just do it!" I scream.

"Listen to her!" Beltz yells, adding to the insanity of the moment, his voice so loud it echoes around the flightdeck. "She knows what she's doing!"

I give the ship thirty percent starboard thrust, moving us away from the next ice wave building in our direction. The boom slides freely in its slot below us. As we move away from the storm, the boom appears to swing toward the coming wave.

"The boom … it's going to get ruined," Jeffers says weakly.

"The boom will be fine. Just watch." I've practiced this twice before. Twice. Not enough to be as confident as I sound, but they'll never know that. The first time in the sim I failed miserably; the second time I mostly succeeded. *Let's hope I improve with practice.*

The ship moves fifty meters to the left, the boom trailing behind and angled to the right, giving the ship enough distance from the storm to allow me to breathe again.

Now that we're free of the immediate danger of the next ice wave, I can continue the uptake of the boom segments. One by one they lock into place until they're completely within the boom chamber, and the door bangs shut behind it. All the red lights and holograms fade out and disappear altogether. I wipe another several drops of sweat from my face.

"Withdrawing from ice-grab," I say before flipping on the all-com and speaking again. "We're done for now. Got about seventy percent full on this grab. We'll try again another time to top off."

I nod at Baebong who's staring at me as if seeing me for the first time.

"Bring us out of atmosphere," I say, nodding at him. "Chart a course to meet up with the DS Mekanika."

He turns around without a word to follow my orders.

I sit back in my seat as the ship starts its ascent and the groaning of its exterior panels lessens. When we're finally on track to head out, I allow myself to relax. My body feels nearly boneless as I sag in my chair. "Holy shit that was close," I whisper to myself.

Baebong hears me and glares at me over his shoulder. "Too close."

A voice instantly recognizable as Rollo's comes over the line. "When's the soonest we can shower, Captain? Rollo had a ... uh ... small accident."

Picturing him pissing his pants, I start giggling and can't stop. All the stress from the danger of that ice-grab is making me feel like my head is going to explode. I bury my face in my hands for a few seconds, trying to get a grip on my runaway emotions. Slowly but surely, my brain empties of thoughts of my near death and that of my crew and I can breathe normally again.

"No one uses the water until the Captain tells you it is permitted." Beltz is using the all-comm to answer Rollo and anyone else who might have the same question he did. After switching it off, he leans down, banging his hand on my shoulder a few times. My hands fall away from my face and rest limply on the arms of the captain's chair.

"Well done," he says with a chuckle. "But I still say you are a crazy bitch. I have never seen anything like that in my life." He laughs louder, apparently thrilled to have looked death in the face and walked away unscathed. Easy for him; it's not his damn ship that needs an overhaul.

I knock his hand off, not angry with him, but because having him touch me in a fatherly way makes me feel like a kid. I don't need his approval or anyone else's. This is my ship and I fly her the way I feel is best. Although, looking back over the last ten minutes, I'm not sure risking everything like I just did was worth the water we took on. *What made me do that? Was I really worried about my crew's hydration needs or was I trying to show off?* I really hope it's the former because show-offs die in the Dark. That's a fact.

Properly subdued by my own gloomy thoughts, I address the ship's computer with more humility that I was feeling thirty seconds ago. "Adelle, I need a full report on the ship's systems and structural stability in two hours. Can you do it?"

"Of course, Captain. I can give it to you in five minutes if you prefer."

"No, thanks. Two hours is good." That gives me time to eat and shower. I need to be clear-headed to deal with the aftermath of this mission. Now I know what I'm up against, at least when it comes to my own ship. As far as the Alliance is concerned, we still have to see about that. I hope it's a lot less precarious a situation than the one we just sneaked our way out of. I feel like I cheated Death himself, and I'm worried he's going to want his due eventually. And like Baebong said … we're too young to die.

CHAPTER
TWENTY-EIGHT

I USED TO TAKE SHOWERS for granted, but never again will I be doing that. *Holy shit, this feels good. Did I die and go to Heaven or what?* The water slides over me, standing out in droplets on my greasy skin where I haven't yet run the cloth covered in dull grey suds. The harsh soap that Lucinda makes with some of her plant materials cuts through the grime nicely but leaves my body feeling like it's burning. I don't care, though. Whatever it takes to get this stink off me, I'm all for it. A freshly washed flightsuit is waiting for me on my bunk. I was happy to find that the ship's cleaning systems actually work pretty well; must be because they were hardly used by Langlade's crew before I came onboard.

The shampoo, also given to me by Lucinda, smells like flowers. I can't place which ones exactly, but I'm thrilled to be smelling like a girl for a change and not a station dump's mongrel. It's weird how my hair feels like it's grown longer in the thirty hours since I've come onboard the DS Anarchy. I think all the grime and knots made it seem shorter than it was.

When I step out of the shower naked and wet, goose-bumps rise up all over my body. My chamber is colder than I'd like, but it's probably for the best. Any warmer in here, and I'd be tempted to lie down in my bunk and sleep for twenty hours at least. There's still business to be taken care of and I won't get it done with my eyes closed.

A voice breaks into my thoughts, and I grab the towel off a nearby hook and hold it against me in response.

"Captain, you awake?"

It's Rollo outside my door. I let the towel go and use it to dry my arms and then my legs. "Yes, I'm awake, Rollo. What is it?"

"Rollo has been instructed to tell you that we are approximately twenty minutes from our destination." Someone yells at him in the background and he sighs before continuing. "Correction. *Thirty* minutes. Jesus, is everyone anal on this ship or what? Anyway, do you want Rollo to bring you some food?"

"No. Everyone meets at the dining table in ten." My eyes scan the room, looking for the things I'll need to get presentable for my crew. There are several closed panels I've yet to open and explore. Maybe one of them holds a drying device and something that will make me look less near-dead than I do now. The mirror in this place is pissing me off. I look like a stowaway pulled off a garbage scow, and I should know since I've seen that face in the mirror before.

"Should Rollo tell them?" he asks.

"No, I'll take care of it." I cut off the comm with him and speak out loud in my room. "Adelle?"

"Yes, Captain?"

"Tell all the crew to meet in the dining room in ten minutes. Attendance is mandatory. They'd better be dead if they're not there."

"Yes, Captain."

Seconds later I hear the faint evidence of Adelle following my order echoing down the corridor outside my door. I hurry to get my flight suit on and run a comb through my hair. "Do I have anything to dry my hair in this chamber?" I ask Adelle.

A panel to my left opens, dropping a drying dome down and bringing a seat out underneath it from another panel. "Yes, Captain. What setting do you prefer?"

"Blast me. I have five minutes to get presentable." I finish sliding into my flight suit, zipping up the jacket and walking over to the dryer.

"As you wish."

Taking a seat below the dome, I begin to shiver as the invisible air currents and dehydrator work to remove the humidity from my hair. All of the moisture will be captured and returned to the filtration system to be used somewhere else; maybe for another shower or for our drinking water. Nothing gets wasted on a DS if the ship's systems are functioning properly. Whether this particular DS is in good enough shape to harvest that water I just used is another question. Now I feel guilty; maybe I should have washed at the sink.

"Adelle, what's our water filtration functionality right now?"

"Eighty-three percent effective, Captain."

"What do we need to fix it and get it to one hundred?" I know one hundred percent functionality is pretty much impossible, but I like to know the best case scenario and work from there.

"I can provide you with a list at your hand unit if you wish. It is quite comprehensive."

I look over at the device that sits on the sink across the room. I'll strap it to my wrist when I leave, so that during the meeting I can be updated by Adelle and communicate with the crew more effectively. I used to avoid the damn things because they reminded me too much of the shock bracelets I've been forced to wear, but I realize now that's a silly thought. It's time for me to grow up and start living in the present instead of dwelling in the past so much. And for the first time in my life, I think I can do it. Something about this drifters' alliance is giving me hope. I just pray it's not totally misplaced and undeserved.

"Fine. Send the list there. Who's in the dining room right now?" I reach up and feel my hair. It's almost completely dry.

"Everyone but you, Captain."

"Lucinda's there?" I'm pleasantly surprised. Glad too, because I didn't want to have to kick her off the ship.

"Yes, Captain."

I'm tempted to ask Adelle to bug the room for me, but I don't. I never liked being spied on by my father and his minions, so I'm not about to do it to someone else. If my crew wants to plan a mutiny, let them. I'll deal with it when it comes up. *If* it comes up.

Who are you kidding? After that ice-grab stunt, everyone's going to want off this ship. I sigh, wondering how in the hell I'm going to manage flying the thing by myself. I'll have to limp over to the nearest waystation and try to recruit a whole new crew with only a promise of future riches. That'll be fun. And by fun, I mean not fun at all.

I push the drying dome off my head, letting it fall back into the wall to be covered by a panel again. The chair follows as I stand and no longer need it. The mirror gives me a better report than it did previously; at least my hair is clean and slightly fluffy, no longer stuck to my head by several weeks' worth of grease.

"Are you ready?" I ask my reflection.

"Am I ready for what?" Adelle asks.

"I'm talking to myself, Adelle. Disregard."

"Yes, Captain. But if I may, I believe you are ready."

I lift my eyes to the ceiling. "Oh yeah?" *Great. A computer with an opinion. How did I get so lucky?*

"Yes. Your mission to extract water from the surface of Xylera was a success. You managed your limited resources to the maximum extent possible without any loss of life. Your water stores are replenished at over fifty percent and your shield is now fully functioning across the entire ship. According to my data, you are ready."

"Ready for what?" I ask, almost laughing. Computers are so stupid sometimes.

"Ready to face the OSG warship approximately eight kilometers from our present position, inbound."

The blood goes cold in my veins. "Did you just say a warship is headed our way?"

"Yes, Captain, I did."

I take off running out of my chamber, tripping over the threshold in the hallway and falling to my knees, making them bloody in the process. I can feel the stinging cut skin below my suit, but there's no time to worry about it now. I need all hands on deck, and before that can happen, I need to know if they even want to be there for me.

CHAPTER
TWENTY-NINE

I STRIDE INTO THE DINING room and take the seat at the head of the table. My crew had started to stand when I entered the room, but they take their seats in confusion when they see I'm not waiting around for the courtesy afforded me.

"I don't see Beltz," I say, irritated that everyone isn't here.

"He's back on his ship," Baebong says. "We joined up when you were in the shower."

I shake my head, wondering why that bothers me. He doesn't belong here, he belongs there on the DS Mekanika. "Where are they now?"

Baebong shrugs. "Around somewhere not far. They're cloaked, so it's kind of hard to tell exactly until they contact us. He said they would soon, to arrange a meeting."

He scratches his head. "Not sure what he was talking about, though. A meeting?"

"Fine." I wave off his unspoken question to address the more serious issue at hand. "We have a problem."

Gus laughs. "Yeah, too much water onboard. I don't know whether to shower myself or wash the engine room down first."

Everyone on the crew chuckles but me, so their joy peters out pretty quickly.

"Sorry to rain on your parade, but we have a warship headed our way, and before they get here, I need to know who's with me and who's not." My fingers wrap around the arms of my chair, digging into the carved wood surface. It's the first time I notice that I'm sitting on actual wood here in the dining room. Langlade apparently liked to spoil himself with rare things while eating.

"A warship?" Rollo looks from one face around him to another. "Is it the same one as before?" He finally settles on staring at me when no one offers up an answer for him.

"I have no idea. I haven't made contact yet. I need to know first who's with me."

Everyone looks at me as though confused.

"We are all with you, Captain," Jeffers finally says, ending the game of silence it felt like we were playing.

"Yeah. Why are you even asking?" Gus looks at me, then at his brother. "Am I missing something?"

"She's just worried she scared you guys away with her ice-grab," Baebong says, cool as hell. Like he wasn't going white in the face and screaming at me like a puff when I told him to release the boom chuck. But I let him have his moment of false bravery and watch as the rest of the crew rushes to affirm their loyalty.

"Worried?" Gus laughs, a little too forcefully. "Nooo, not at all. Like Beltz said, that was the work of a finely tuned machine. You've obviously earned the captain's chair." Gus nods first at me and then at everyone else around the table.

"Never seen anything like it," Rollo says. "And Rollo has seen a lot, you can trust Rollo on that."

"You get your pants cleaned?" I ask, trying not to smile.

He looks down at his lap and then back up at me. "Rollo spilled some tea on himself. It's not a big deal."

"Sure you did." I turn my attention to Jeffers as the crew laughs. "We good for food?"

"Never better," he says, grinning. "I have something special planned for our next meal. I understand we'll be having guests."

I nod, looking at all the faces before me, at the people who've decided to throw their lot in with mine, come hell or high icy waters. I can't lie; it's pretty damn amazing to feel the way I do right now. I can't remember ever being this proud. And now it's time to up the ante, to see if they really are in this with me through thick and thin.

"We've been invited to join a drifters' alliance. I don't know all the details yet, but with us, they'd number five."

"What's an alliance of only five DSs going to do for us?" Tam asks.

"An excellent question. We'll find out the answer to that question and any others we have over a meal with Beltz and his crew."

"When?" Baebong asks.

"As soon as we get the hell away from this warship."

"We going to do evasive maneuvers?" Gus asks. He sounds way too happy about the prospect.

"I sincerely hope not," I say, still wasted from my last adrenaline overdose. The closest planet being Xylera does not bode well for an evasive escape. I'm not good enough to fly around moving ice waves; even I can admit that much.

"What if they want to board us?" Lucinda asks.

"Better get your stink machine going," I say, winking at her.

She has the decency to go a little red in the cheeks. Hopefully that'll be the last trick she tries to play on me.

"Seriously," I say, no longer messing around with her. "Do whatever you can to make the biogrid seem inhospitable to strangers. I don't want anyone going beyond the antechamber into the grid itself."

"What about the disk?" Baebong asks.

"Where is it?" I look around at my crew, wondering who took charge of it when I became incapacitated.

"I buried it," Lucinda says.

I grip the edges of my seat a little less forcefully and look at everyone, knowing I'm trusting them with everything I have to my name. Going against a warship is one thing; going against its crew while it's onboard *this* ship is a whole other mess of giant proportions. That's personal, and you never know who a crew member is connected to usually until it's too late.

I measure my words carefully, knowing that I'm saying so much more than their simplest translation. "If we have to, we bring the disk out. Jens said it makes some people sick. People like I used to be. People who are part of the OSG machine. Those affected by that disk today, if we bring it out, won't be people who broke away and tried to forge their own lives. They'll be true believers in the OSG realpolitik. You don't get on the crew of a warship without being a disciple."

The whole idea of going up against people like that makes a shiver go up and down my spine. I feel as though

I'll be signing not only my own death warrant, but those of my crew too. I know better than anyone the power OSG officials can wield when the spirit moves them to do so. Before, my decisions only affected me. Now, they affect all these good people too. I had no idea the stress that would be put on me when I was dreaming of being the captain of a DS.

"But what if they don't have chips in their backs like you did?" Rollo asks. "Or what if some do and some don't? We'll get fried if some of them start dropping like flies and others don't. They'll know something's up."

"I'll worry about that when it happens." I give him a special glare that says what I'm thinking, namely: *Thanks, Rollo, for that glimpse into a possible horror show I hadn't yet considered.* "For now, leave the disk where it is. But if you hear me say the word *Hallelujah*, bring it out. Put it on the flightdeck somewhere."

I wait for Lucinda to nod and indicate that she understands, which she does without hesitation. Her expression is decidedly more cooperative-looking now. I hope it lasts longer than my hairstyle does this time.

"Captain," Adelle's voice interrupts my next thought, "you are being contacted by the WS Baltimore."

"I'll be right there." To my crew I say, "Are we all good?"

Everyone nods.

"Thank you. Back to your stations."

"What about Rollo?" Rollo asks.

"Rollo, you come with me."

We'll see how good a bargainer this guy is. If we get into a position to negotiate and he blows it by pissing off someone on that warship, I can afford to hand him over to the OSG as payment for sins committed. If he doesn't, I'll let him stay. Trial by fire is the surest way to find out the measure of a person. This I know from first-hand experience.

CHAPTER THIRTY

EVERYONE IS IN PLACE ON the flightdeck before I respond to the reach attempt by the WS Baltimore.

"We ready?" I ask.

Baebong, Rollo, and Jeffers nod, all of them staring up at the clearpanel that will soon show our caller.

I accept the reach. "Warship Baltimore, this is Captain Cass of the DS Anarchy, we accept your reach with visual elements."

The clearpanel flickers and the face of a man I am familiar with appears. He's in full battledress uniform, and he's sporting a new scar I don't remember seeing before. It cuts across his nose and his left cheek. Knowing him, he said no to MI because he thinks it makes him look sexy or something. He always did have a pretty high opinion of himself.

"Captain Cass, this is Captain Terrick Overshine. Thank you for accepting our reach. Feel free to share visual element as well."

You wish. Easiest way to identify me, and not going to happen. "I'm having a bad hair day," I say, locking out the visual element so it can't be accessed by anyone. "So if you don't mind, I'd rather keep it to voice only."

"Suit yourself. We understand that you attempted an ice-grab on Xylera. This after being told you could not do so without paying the tariff."

I take two long breaths in an attempt to keep my tone even. How dare they tell me I can't get water when I need it. *Someone wants a hole punched into his hull, I know that.* My training kicks in without conscious thought once again, keeping my temper from my voice. "I don't know where you heard that, Captain, because that's not the case."

"We saw you accessing the surface."

Now he's just pissing me off. I mute the comm and talk loud enough for my crew to hear me. "Fuck you and the warship you rode in on, Overshine." Then I un-mute, opening the channel to him again, and smile sweetly. "What you saw, actually, was us taking a break from all the junk flying around the atmosphere out here. Is that you letting off all that waste crystal?" He and I both know it's against regulations to dump waste in this part of the galaxy, but does that stop assholes like him from doing it when no one's looking? Hell no. Do as I say, not as I do. That's the OSG way.

"It is against regulations to release waste into the Dark near any planet known to host life forms or atmosphere conducive to such."

"Yeah. I know," I deadpan. Now he knows I was accusing him, and I know he's full of shit. Not that I saw any waste crystals out there, but I know his reputation. He's not a by-the-book kind of guy.

"We'd like to board your ship and check for contraband," he says.

I laugh. "And I'd like to board your ship and do the same. But I can't and neither can you."

"Regulation 34 dash 1891 says that any ship suspected of carrying contraband items may be boarded by …"

"Yeah, yeah, yeah," I say, cutting him off, "…but you don't have a valid suspicion, do you?"

"As a matter of fact, we do."

"Oh yeah? What is it? Because regulations also say you have to notify me of that suspicion and its basis before boarding."

"You were dock-linked with a known smuggler of contraband items."

I mute the comm and punch my fist down on the arm of my chair. "Dammit!" He totally has me. The regs are clear in this area. I look around, searching for ideas. "Fucking Beltz."

"Parts dealers always get jammed for that," Rollo says. "It's total bullshit." He shakes his head in disappointment.

I spark up the comm again. "I'm not sure who you're referring to." Now I'm just stalling for time, and Overshine's going to know it. But I need to figure out my exit strategy. Xylera is not the planet for evasive maneuvers. If I try to run, we'll die, and I'm not going down that way; not with Overshine as my grim reaper. He's not worth it, the sniveling, ass-kissing prick I remember from my childhood. He was five years ahead of me in our training squadron, so he didn't know I existed, but that didn't stop me from seeing every move he made, every skull he cracked, and every rule he broke to get to the top. He's twenty-four and already commanding a warship? He has to have at least thirty notches in his belt.

"The DS Mekanika," he says. His voice rings out like a death knell.

"Never heard of it," I say right away. Probably too fast. I know better than to let deceit enter my voice, and yet I did it. *Fucking Overshine. Dammit again!*

"We saw you docked together," he says, bored and annoyed with my obvious lies.

"No you didn't."

"We're coming aboard, Cass."

"That's Captain Cass to you, asshole." I shut off the comm, simultaneously cutting their reach.

The comm screen goes blank and then the clearpanel is back up. The warship is there, filling up the entire frame.

"Holy shit, that mother is big," Baebong says. "I've never seen one that close up before."

I flip the all-comm switch and speak carefully. I'm exhausted and worried that it's showing in my voice. "Prepare to be boarded by crew members of the Warship Baltimore. Protect our assets. Get ready to sing Hallelujah."

I turn to face Rollo. "Rollo, my friend, now it's your turn."

"Rollo's turn? Rollo's turn for what?"

"Rollo's turn to show me he's worth keeping around and not better off being traded for a pass to the Warship Baltimore." Not that I'd trade him off as a battle practice dummy, which is what he'd end up serving as, but he doesn't know that.

Rollo stands, wiping his hands down the legs of his pants. "Rollo is ready. All he needs is a bargaining chip."

"Go talk to Lucinda. See what she has that won't give our biogrid away."

He takes off running from the flightdeck, and I turn my head to look out the clearpanel again.

"Are we going to jail?" Baebong asks. "Because I didn't sign up for that when I joined this crew. I really didn't. I won't do well in jail. I'm too pretty."

I sigh, long and loudly. "No one's going to jail." *Not now anyway.* Not as long as I have anything to say about it. My mind works feverishly to come up with something I can use to bargain with against the lackey Overshine will surely send to search my ship.

CHAPTER THIRTY-ONE

THE SOUND OF SEVERAL PAIRS of boots coming down the corridor connecting our airlock to that of the warship is ominous. I've heard it in my nightmares. Hell, I used to be one of the crew that made those noises, and the memories will be enough to fuel my darkest dreams for a lifetime. I want to believe my past can stay were it belongs, but here it is again, surfacing to torture me once more. I'm afraid I'll never get fully away from it no matter how far I fly.

The lead person on the boarding crew is a stranger to me — a girl with short black hair, maybe five centimeters taller than I am, and trained at least to Level Four. I can tell by the way she walks what her skills probably are, and her strength by the muscles showing in her arms and outlined through her pants. She's proud of herself, ready for action in her sleeveless jacket. Pretty stupid, though, because I could filet that skin of hers with a lot less effort when she's dressed this way. Vanity: it's a weakness I especially enjoy exploiting. I turn my attention away from her, effectively letting her know that she means nothing to me. No threat. I could take her down without blinking an eye.

Next in line are two guys. They're older, more battle scarred than the pretty girl in front. They carry weapons across their chests, making no bones about the fact that this encounter could get real ugly, real quick if I don't keep their captain happy. Them, I take more seriously.

Next in line is the man himself. I'm a little surprised that Overshine came onboard personally, but maybe I shouldn't be. Cass isn't the most common name in the universe. Maybe he came to see for himself if I'm the same Cass who went missing from the OSG's clutches three years ago. Nothing in his expression gives him away, though. His face could be carved from Ventilian rock with how hard it appears.

Behind him are two more crew members, these guys younger, closer in age to Baebong and myself. I don't recognize them from my old station, so I assume they were trained elsewhere in the galaxy. They also carry weapons, although not as confidently as their elders. They aren't worth any more of my attention than they've already received, so I look again at Overshine. He's the one I need to worry about; he holds all the cards in this game. Most of them anyway. I might have one or two up my sleeve. *We'll see.*

I stand with my hands hanging at my sides, ready for any sudden moves on their part, but appearing casual as I take in the details of this posse. The girl in front lifts her chin at me, her eyes glittering with a hatred I realize is born from the propaganda she's been swallowing her entire life. I know what it's all about because I've eaten from the same bowl she has. The difference between the two of us is that I looked down at the meal and saw what it was made up of; she closes her eyes when she spoons it into her stupid maw.

"Captain Cass of the DS Kinsblade, I presume," she says.

I look over her shoulder and address the man with the real power. "Captain Overshine. Welcome aboard. Please instruct your crew to leave their weapons in the airlock. You're welcome to use your side of it if you don't like the idea of us having access to them." My insult is clear. *You scared, Overshine? Because I think you are. Otherwise you wouldn't need so much firepower surrounding you.*

His eyes flicker, but I'm not sure if it's with recognition or irritation. Maybe it's a little of both.

No one moves. Rollo, Jeffers, and Baebong are at my back. Lucinda is busy stinking up her chambers to discourage too much investigation, and the twins are remaining scarce. I told them to be ready for anything when I passed by the engine room earlier on my way here.

"My crew will not use their weapons unless provoked."

I shrug. "Your crew will not pass onto my ship with those weapons in their possession. My ship, my rules. You have no authority here. I'm allowing you access as a courtesy, nothing more." I bow slightly to show him I don't mean to embarrass him in front of his troops. But the rules are what they are; mere suspicion of wrongdoing is not enough to permit weaponry onboard an otherwise friendly ship.

He steps forward, his crew parting to the sides as he advances. He stops just beside the girl. For the first time, I see her gaze lose some of its confidence. Either she doubts herself now or she's scared of him. If I had to guess, I'd say it's a bit of both going on there. I remember fearing him getting too close to me back in the day. He was prone to fits of temper and lashing out, if I recall correctly.

"The rules have changed, Captain Cass."

"Not according to me they haven't."

"Fortunately for us, you aren't the one making them." He looks over his shoulder at his crew. "Board the ship. Check their water levels."

"Water is not contraband," I say, getting more irritated by the second as the two older men still with their weapons move past me and over to the nearest keypad.

Overshine's expression remains impassive. "It is if you don't pay the tariff."

The guy at the keypad looks over at me. "I'm locked out."

"Unlock it." Overshine stares down at me with so much confidence in his face I can't stand it; I want to punch him right in the jaw. I'd make it count, too. One shot. That's all I'd need to lay him out and use him as a doormat. It's only the respect I have for my own crew's right of self-determination —namely the means by which they will die one day— that keeps me from following through on that desire.

I speak low enough so only he can hear me. "Fuck you, Overshine."

He looks up and addresses his men. "Captain Cass has offered to show me the water stores herself. Wait here." He takes me by the elbow and forces me out of the airlock area and into the cargo bay.

Baebong attempts to follow us, but two guns come up to stop him, blocking his path.

"Wait there," I say over my shoulder as I'm pushed into a corridor. "I'll be right back." I have to practically run to keep from being dragged along.

"Resisting is not a good idea," Overshine says in a quieter tone. There might even be a trace of humility there, but it's more likely that my ears deceive me. I remember watching some of his training sessions. He's nothing but ruthless, even when it's not necessary to be that way to get the job done. I remember hating that about him back when I was a part of that OSG machine. The memories are like a bitterness on my tongue that I cannot swallow away. I can't believe this ass cheese is touching me without my permission. He's going to pay for that.

"Forcing me against my *will* is a bad idea," I say, yanking my arm out of his grasp. I continue walking down the corridor, though, because he's got friends pointing particle rays at my people. If someone dies because I was being stubborn, I'll never forgive myself.

Showing him our water is a foregone conclusion, I realize that now. But the interpretation that I offer for what he sees and whether I can convince him of the truth of that interpretation remains to be seen. I channel all the bullshitting capabilities I have and focus on them in my brain. *Sell him the idea that you didn't just sneak more than half a megaliter of water from right under his nose. Convince him. Distract him. Get him thinking about something else.*

I change my stride to one with a little sway to it and be sure to position myself in front of him. Using my sexuality was never something I was trained to do with the OSG, but I'm no idiot. Heat works. I've lived on my own for three years, sometimes in the roughest places in the universe, and I survived intact — but not by playing the innocent, that's for sure. Innocents get taken down, but women who look like they know what they're doing are respected out here in the Dark. I'll do whatever it takes short of giving away my very last gift to get rid of this guy and his crew so we can be on our way to making contact with the Alliance. An alliance that's looking better and better by the minute.

CHAPTER
THIRTY-TWO

W E STOP AT THE KEYPAD by my chambers, the first door we come to after leaving the airlocks and cargo bay area.

"What's the access code?" he asks, his hand hovering over the numbers and letters as he waits for my response.

I laugh, knocking his hand away. "Yeah, right." I press the button on the keypad that will allow access to our system information panel and open my palm to hold it in front of the sensor as I stare him down. "You really think I'm an idiot, don't you?"

"Access granted," says Adelle's voice.

"I do, as a matter of fact," he says, his face once again a mask of zero emotion.

He's being so cold and emotionless, it's weird. If I didn't know better, I'd think he was a compubot wearing an

Overshine kit to make him look like the boy from my past life. Objectively, I could see why someone would want to do that; he is pretty easy on the eyes. But subjectively, no way could I understand why anyone would want to use Overshine as a model for a compubot kit. Why dress a compubot up to look like a depraved psycho?

"Show water storage level," I say to Adelle, refusing to break eye contact with my oppressor. "If you think I'm an idiot, then you're not nearly as smart as I thought you were." I'm being extra generous, since I really don't think he's that smart at all.

A grid shows up on the small screen above the keypad displaying our water stores. I look at it to confirm what I already know as Adelle reads what's there aloud. "Water levels at sixty-nine percent."

I lift an eyebrow at him. "Sixty-nine percent. And what kind of asshole would I be to risk an ice grab right under your nose without going the full hundred percent?" I press the no-access button and place my hand over the sensor again, shutting down the system so no more information can be shared.

"Like I said — I don't credit you with a lot of brain power. You left the OSG, didn't you?"

So he knows who I am, then. Good. At least now it's out in the open. And I know he knows, and he knows that I know. *So what does this mean? Is he going to report my position? Keep me here until my father shows up to drag me back?* I'll fucking run him through with my knife before I let that happen. I can't believe Overshine let me keep my weapon on me, actually. He knows what I can do with it. *Talk about stupid.* Training at the OSG must be slipping. Or maybe his promotion has gone to his head. He always did strut around a lot whenever he passed a training level.

I look him up and down, sneering when I'm done. "You know, that was always your problem, Overshine. Your head is so fucking big you can hardly fit it through the portals on a warship. I'm surprised you got a seat on the flightdeck, actually. Do they give you a special chair to help you hold that head of yours up off your shoulders? Give your back a break now and again?"

He shoves me by my shoulder, slamming me into the frame of my portal door. "You'd better watch your mouth, *Captain*." He practically spits the last word out as he comes closer, crowding me.

"Why? What are you going to do about it?" A memory of him almost beating the last breath out of a friend of mine, a girl half his size, makes the bile run up into my throat from my stomach. "You going to kill me? Punch me in the temple so many times it turns my brain to mush?" My hand slides down to my leg and my fingers lightly touch the handle of my knife.

"No."

"No?" He's inches away from me, his hot breath smelling of herbs for some reason and heating up my face. "What then? Tell your monkeys to blast my crew? Leave me here to die alone?"

"No," he says, softer this time, staring at me like he's trying to see into my soul. *Ick.* I don't want a slug like him poking around in there.

"What then?" The suspense is killing me. *Why is he standing so close?* If he gets any nearer, we'll be swapping spit, and fuck all if I'm not sweating again in my clean flightsuit. So much for smelling like a girl. My next words come blurting out of my mouth without a filter there to stop them. "You gonna kiss me?"

He backs away, looking confused and maybe even nervous. "No."

I laugh, freaked out about the fact that I might have actually read his mind. "Scared you didn't I?" *Fuck, I scared myself.* I'm sweating double-time now.

"No." His frustration level is going into overdrive, but does that stop me? Hell no. I'm having too much fun to be smart now. This bully who used to lord his superior strength over my friends and me isn't so tough anymore when it's just the two of us standing in the corridor of *my* ship. Some kind of weird adrenaline-like chemical is flooding my system, making me talk way too much.

"Yeah, I figured. Scared of girls too. Scared of us on the practice mat, scared of us in the bedroom." My chin goes up. "I always saw right through you, you know that? Pretty boy on the outside, black as the Dark inside." I sneer. "You disgust me." I take a step to move around him, but he blocks my path.

"Who the hell do you think you are?" He grabs my arm and forces me back. I trip a little over one of his giant boots and my back hits the doorframe again.

"Ow! That hurts!" I yank my arm away from him. "Quit pushing me around!"

He grabs a handful of my hair near my ear and yanks on it. Leaning in, he growls his words in my face. "I'm going to do a lot worse than push you around if you don't shut your mouth."

I reach up to wipe my face. "Say it, don't spray it, plonk."

The hold he has on my hair loosens. "Are you kidding me?" He's back to being confused.

"I just took a shower, all right? I don't need you splattering your sexually frustrated words all over my face." I stand up straighter and pull my jacket down, pretending he's wrinkled it when I know better. It's just that he's gotten me a bit ruffled on the inside, and I need a few seconds to think. I look down at my hands as they smooth out the uncreased material of my jacket, and I have to work at getting back to equilibrium. *What's wrong with me? Why am I baiting him like this?*

"I'm not sexually frustrated," he finally says.

"I really don't want to know, okay?" I laugh and look up at him, now back on two feet after hearing the lack of confidence in his tone. "Your business is yours and mine is mine. So, what do you say we go our separate ways and pretend this never happened?"

His voice goes cold. "I'm telling him where you are."

Does this mean the picochip wasn't a locator? I'm not sure if that's good news or bad news.

"Him who?" Every ounce of calm I have left in my body and brain is funneled into those words. It's almost good enough to fool even me that I'm that clueless. *Him.* Of course I know who he's referring to.

"Him, your father. As if you didn't know." He's back to being a tough guy. I guess my attempt at being cool was a total bust.

I shrug. "So. Tell him whatever you want. I don't give a floating crystallized shit flake and neither does he."

"You sure about that?"

Something in his eyes tells me he knows a hell of a lot better than I do what my father thinks, feels, and wants. My father could be his commanding officer for all I know. The panic starts to take over at the very idea. I've worked for so long, so tirelessly for three years to keep my independence, and this guy could end that right now just by being in a bad mood.

"Fuck you, Overshine." The words come out kind of choked. Then some very irritating and inconvenient tears appear in the corners of my eyes. I tip my head back to try and make them go away. "Rrrrr … fuck!" I swipe at my face, hoping he'll pretend along with me that it's sweat dripping down my cheeks.

We stand there, the two of us, just staring at one another. He looks angry, and I know I'm pissed. I want to cut him so bad, but I know that'll just make my situation worse. My hand is shaking with the effort of staying away from my dagger.

"What do you want?" I finally say, clearing my throat to get rid of the lump in it.

"What do I want?" He looks surprised.

"Yeah. That's what I said. What do you want?"

His eyebrows draw together. "What exactly are you asking?"

I hiss out a long breath. "You can't really be that dense, can you?" I shift my weight over to one leg. "You're the captain of a warship. Tell me you know how to negotiate."

"Oh, I know you're trying to negotiate. I just don't know what it is you're offering." He still looks mad. It's strange to see a person getting pissed about a potential trade; that's a new one for me, especially considering what I'm offering.

I lift my chin. "What do you want?"

He steps closer. "There's only one thing on this ship that I want."

The way he's staring down at me, I'm pretty sure I know what he's referring to, but I just can't believe it. He never expressed that kind of interest in me or anyone else I ever knew. He was always too focused on clawing and beating his way to the top to think about people as potential sleepmates. I always got the impression that he saw everyone as his next potential beatdown victim.

"And what would that be?" I say, cool as can be.

"Guess."

"Water?" I hate that my tone is so meek.

His hand comes up and rests on the wall behind me, near the side of my head. His tone goes warmer. "No, it's not water. I'm at full capacity."

Or maybe I'm just imagining that tone in his voice. Warm is never a word one would use to describe Terrick Overshine. I'm falling into panic mode now and blurt out the first thing I think of.

"Nuts? We have some nuts we traded for before. We could give those to you." Hopefully Beltz will forgive the fact that I'm trading his nuts away. *Please let Overshine want my nuts.*

"No. It's not nuts that I want."

Dammit. No nuts. I shrug, trying to appear casual. "Sorry, but that's about all we have of value on this ship."

He shakes his head but says nothing. The heat between us is rising. *Panic, panic, panic...*

He can't possibly mean *me*, though. *Right? Right?!* This is just a game he's playing to mess with my head. It has to be. He was around me for years and years and never once acknowledged my existence, unless you count that one time he went after Drake Borgland, the guy who dogged me with a sucker punch when I was bent over to help a comrade in arms. It was kind of impressive how Overshine gave the kid a compound fracture in his right arm right there on the mat, but I always wrote it off as him teaching his teammate a valuable lesson in fair play.

"No, there's something else of value here," he assures me. Then he chuckles. "And it ain't nuts."

"Where?" I look to my left and right, barely missing brushing his nose with mine in the process.

"Captain!" comes a voice from down the corridor.

Overshine stands up straight and moves back away from me, his gaze darting for a split second toward his approaching crew member. That's when I realize he's nervous about being caught standing so close to me. He must be ill; it's the only excuse for him showing any emotion other than supreme confidence.

It makes me feel powerful, like maybe I do have a bargaining chip I can use. The question is, how far will it get me? Because if I'm right about what he's hinting at, it's the kind of chip you can only really use once.

"Yes, Lieutenant?" Overshine clasps his hands behind his back as his crew member walks around the corner.

"We're getting a call from the flightdeck that needs your attention, Sir."

Overshine nods once. "I'll be right there. Prepare to disengage with the DS Kinsblade."

"Yes, Sir." The guy jogs back down the corridor toward the airlocks, leaving us standing there alone again. The particles between us are charged enough that they send my heart racing.

"It's the DS Anarchy now," I say in a rush. My nostrils flare as I force my mouth shut in an effort to control myself. I want this guy gone, but then again, I wish I knew what had almost passed between us. It's very frustrating to be so confused about a situation; usually I'm pretty clear about what I'm doing and what other people mean when they say things to me, even when they're talking around a subject and not coming right out and saying what they mean. I want to stab him *and* I want to talk to him, ask him what he's all about. Ask him what happened in his training after I left. I must be crazy.

"You named your ship the DS Anarchy?" His eyebrow goes up.

"Yep." I nod to add to the strength of my conviction.

The corner of his mouth quirks up for a brief moment and then the emotion disappears as quickly as it arrived and he becomes a steeloid wall again. "Figures."

I shrug. "What can I say? Subtlety is not one of my strong points."

"Could have fooled me." He steps forward without another word, takes my chin in his hand, and leans down, pressing his lips against mine.

Shock. Surprise. Fear. Loathing. Breathlessness. *Ack!* I feel all of these things at the exact same time in one big wave of emotion and physical sensation. I wasn't prepared for it. That's my excuse for not stabbing him in the eyeball right away. I'm too stunned to compute exactly what's happening. *He despises me but he kisses me? In what galaxy does that make sense?* Not in the Triangulum, that's for sure.

Thankfully, even though my brain is offline, my instinct is not; I slide my dagger free and bring it up to the side of his neck to rest at his pulse. His lips break free but hover just above mine.

I'm surprised how calm and cool I can speak, all things considered. "Back away, Overshine, really fucking slowly, or I'm going to open up your carotid artery and let you bleed out in front of my bedroom door."

He leans away five centimeters and stares down into my eyes, not a single ounce of fear showing there. "That's your bedroom in there?" His gaze flicks to his left.

I nod, pressing the knife in harder. It pricks his skin, drawing blood.

"Too bad you didn't let me know that sooner." And then, without another word, he stands and backs away, taking a square of cloth from his pocket to press against his bleeding neck. The cocky asshole is back, and I see the same guy I saw bashing people on the mat all those years ago. But then again, I don't see the same guy anymore. Now he's someone totally different — a guy who kissed me for no damn good reason that I can come up with. *Oh well.* Doesn't matter. He's an OSG disciple and I'm not. *Goodbye, Overshine. Don't let the airlock door hit you on the ass on the way out. No wait … on second thought … go ahead and let it.*

Now that all is right with my world, I can stop acting like a brainless twink. I wipe his blood off on my pant leg and slide the knife back into its sheath at my thigh.

"I'm letting you go this time, Cass," he says, walking backward down the corridor, practically strutting. "It's not going to happen a second time."

"Please." I snort. "I'm letting *you* go." I'm making no sense, but whatever. I have to say something because I'm not going to stand here like a little girl mooning over a kiss from a cute guy. He's the enemy, not boyfriend material. And even if he were boyfriend material, I wouldn't be interested.

"You need to stay away from the water sources," he says. And I could swear I see an emotion flicker across his face that I know doesn't appear there very often: sadness. But a half a second later it's gone making me think I probably just imagined it.

"Yeah, sure," I say bitterly. "I'll stay away from the water, as soon as I figure out how to survive without it."

"I'm not kidding. He's looking for you. He knows you'll have to show up eventually."

I say nothing to that. Just the idea of that man coming for me makes me physically ill. A burning starts in my stomach and spreads from there. I'm too angry and scared to face the situation head on, to say what needs to be said to Terrick Overshine in the face of his threat. Instead, I place my shaking hand over the keypad, open the door to my room, and quickly step inside, letting it close behind me. I slide to the floor as my entire body starts to shake and my legs go out beneath me.

He's after me. He's looking for me. And now, thanks to Overshine, he'll know where I am, who I'm with, and what I'm flying. I am so totally and completely screwed. The only light at the end of the very dark tunnel I see in front of me is the Alliance. More eyes, more ears, and the best chance I have at getting away from the one person I swore I never wanted to see again.

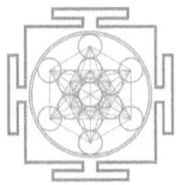

CHAPTER
THIRTY-THREE

I'M SITTING AT THE HEAD of my dining table, which has been extended to admit three additional guests: Captain Beltz, Jens Beltz, and Jacov last name unknown. Everyone's waiting for me to be the first one to break the bread. And when Jeffers told me that was the case, I hadn't realized he meant it literally.

"This bread is as hard as a rock," I say, straining to take a piece from the end of the loaf we're supposed to share.

"Give it to me," Beltz says, taking it from my hand. He whacks it on the edge of the table between us like it's some kind of ion saber meant to cut the table in two. Everyone jumps as a thousand crumbs and a huge chunk from the end of the loaf fly up into the air and rain down on our plates.

I lean over and snatch my piece from the air just before it falls into a bowl of carrots.

"Good catch," Jens says. "You have great reflexes." He's staring at my chest. Again.

Baebong slaps him on the back of the head. "Head out of the waste pipe, germ."

Jens ducks down and scowls at his empty dish.

"Welcome to my table," I say to our guests and my crew, trying to bring a modicum of solemnity back into the room. "And thank you for sharing your food with us." I hold up the rock that's supposed to be my share of the bread.

Gus hides a snort of laugher in the back of his hand and then jumps when his brother nudges him in the ribs with his elbow.

"We're grateful to you also for the trade you made us yesterday for the boom chuck." I grin like a girl who barely escaped the clutches of Death, which I'm pretty sure I did. "Worked like a charm."

"We're lucky it didn't get frozen off," Baebong mumbles.

"That was not luck," Beltz says in a booming voice. "That was skill."

"Thank you, Beltz." I nod at him regally.

"Call me Gunter." He winks at me and wiggles his eyebrows a little.

"How come she gets to call you Gunter?" Jens asks.

"Shut up, boy. Eat your carrots." Gunter doesn't spare his cousin even a glance. His eyes are on me. "Tell us, Captain Cass. What is your plan for the future?"

I look around at all my crew members and the stowaway who has yet to prove his worth to me, taking in the fearful and questioning expressions I see on all of their faces. I never appreciated before the tremendous responsibility I would have as captain of a DS. I'm not regretting my decision to play that hand of givit, but I am wondering if I'm really good enough, tough enough, and smart enough to do this job.

"Well, we have a decision to make." I fold my hands and rest them on the table in front of my plate full of crumbs. "As you now know, the OSG has changed its focus from that of colonizing the habitable planets of the Triangulum Galaxy to one of resource management."

"More like resource control," Lucinda says, scowling.

"Changing the rules to suit themselves," Rollo adds.

"Exactly. They seek to control our access to water. Today it's water, but who knows what it'll be tomorrow?" I look around at the concerned people before me. "I don't know about any of you, but this doesn't come as a surprise to me."

"You *knew* they were going to do this?" Gus asks.

"No, not exactly. But I spent over ten years training to be a part of the defense forces for the OSG, and based on what I learned, I would say they are more than prepared to fight and fight hard. You don't set up a defense force like that unless you expect to run into some pretty serious resistance. And where else would that resistance come from if not people like us?"

"You never mentioned you were part of the OSG to me," Baebong says, the accusation lacing his words with bitterness.

"You never asked." I shrug, acting like that should be enough. But when he glares back at me, I know I won't be able to walk away with just that between us. I sigh, hating the fact that I have to confess something that seems like it should have nothing to do with my life anymore.

"Perhaps if you just share how you ended up getting from there to here," Jeffers suggests. He gives me a warm smile that I know is designed to make me feel more comfortable, but all it does is slather on the guilt. I should have said something to Baebong before. He deserved that instead of having to hear it at this table. I look at him as I speak, hoping he sees this as the apology it is.

"My father is First Major General Valemar Kennedy of the Omega Systems Group Defense Station, Elite Command."

There are some gasps of recognition and then fear around the table, but I ignore those, focusing only on my best friend. He hasn't moved a muscle, so I can't tell if he even knows of my father.

"I was brought into training at the age of six. Earlier, actually, but that training was done at home. It wasn't officially started until I was the legal age to enter."

"They start training at *six* years of age? That's wild." I look over to see Jens shaking his head and smiling.

I find it sad that he seems to admire their tactics. Lucky for him he's so sheltered that he can afford to spare that emotion. People who've been forced to be a part of it know better. "Don't be impressed, Jens. It's no life for a kid."

His smile disappears in an instant. "No, of course not. I didn't mean anything by it."

"What about your mother?" asks Jeffers, doing a great job of pulling the attention away from Jens's embarrassment. "Was she part of the command as well?"

I shake my head. "No. She wasn't." I'm not willing to say any more about her, so I quickly move on with a more self-directed explanation.

"My training was rigorous. Tough. I rose up through the ranks to Level Ten by the age of fifteen."

"I still do not believe that," Gunter says. His eyes are gleaming, though. I think he'd like to fight me just to see if it's true, but I'm not about to hold another knife to his throat. I don't like treating my friends like that, and I consider him a friend now. *Kind of.*

I go back to focusing on Baebong. "I was officially part of the peacekeeping defense forces, but my father's idea of peacekeeping is very different from mine. To reach Level Ten, I had to enter and win a fight to the death."

"Did you win?" Rollo asks.

Lucinda rolls her eyes.

It's not nearly as stupid a question as it seems, so I answer him. "Nearly."

"Nearly?" Gus laughs, but it's the nervous kind. "What does that mean? You turn your opponent into a droid or what?"

I shake my head. "No. It means I left him needing a lot of MI to get back to functionality again." I'll never get the image of that guy out of my head — a boy who'd been a good friend to me for most of my life, bleeding out on the mat, looking up at me as his eyes went from desperate to glassy.

"So... are you officially Level *Ten* or still Level *Nine*?" Gus asks suspiciously.

"Jesus H Droidman, would you just *leave* it?" Tam asks, disgusted with his brother.

"What?" Gus looks first at Tam and then at the group. "What'd I say?"

"Anyway," I say in a loud voice, trying to move the conversation along, "I left. I'd had enough by the time I turned sixteen, and so I hitched a ride out of there the day of my birthday."

"Where'd you go?" Jens asks, his carrots forgotten.

"Around. Different stations, mostly. Some ships. Worked in a goatherd's biodome for a while shoveling shit."

"Nice," Gus says, nodding and smiling. "Our captain is a former brownshins."

Tam shakes his head as his hand leaves the table slowly. Two seconds later Gus jumps up and turns on his brother, rocking halfway out of his chair. "What the hell, man! Did you just stab me with your fork?!"

"What did you expect, synth brain? She's telling her fucking story and you're jacking her!"

"I'm not jacking her, I'm just saying she's come a long way!" Gus turns to me, his face bright red, making his spots stand out against his skin. "You know that, right, Captain? I have all the respect in the world for you." He puts his hand over his heart and gives me a slight bow.

I nod. "Relax. You're fine." I look at Tam. "I appreciate you watching out for me."

Tam nods and puts his fork back on the table. Gus snatches it away and sits on it, shoving his brother away when he tries to retrieve it.

"I would like to say a few words," Jeffers says.

I wait for him to continue, happy to give the floor to someone else.

"First, thank you, Captain, for sharing what must have been a difficult experience with this group of near strangers on this our first flight together."

I nod. It wasn't nearly as difficult as I'd thought it would be. I can't tell if Baebong has forgiven me, but at least he's not looking at me like I'm dead to him anymore.

"We all have parts of our history that we might like to forget or pretend never existed, but I think it's important to remember that those experiences shape who we are today. And, I, for one, am happy to be a part of your crew. You've proven yourself to be resilient, tough, graceful under pressure, and fair. We can't ask for anything more from our captain."

Everyone but Lucinda nods. She stares off into the distance, and I can't tell if she's even listening to what's being said. I don't hold it against her, though; I remember what it was like to have someone drone on and on about something I didn't believe in.

"Well said, healer," Rollo adds. "Rollo isn't one for drifting normally, but even he'd consider a mission or two if Captain Cass were at the helm."

Baebong stares at him and then turns to look at me.

"What about you, friend?" I say to him, my vulnerability on show for everyone at the table. I can't keep the pleading tone out of my voice. "You still onboard for a mission or two?"

Baebong's eyebrows flicker before he answers. "You still going to let me rig the ship with my weapons?"

I shrug. "As long as the twins assure me you won't blow the place up."

The three of them look at each other and nod. I'm not sure I like the sneaky smiles I see lighting up their faces right now, but there will be plenty of time to deal with that later.

"Okay, so …," Gunter rubs his hands together, "now that we have the nice love fest here at the table, perhaps you can discuss your participation in the Alliance." He crushes a hunk of bread off the loaf with his bare hand and drops it onto his plate before passing the loaf on to Jacov.

"What's this all about?" Lucinda asks. "What Alliance?"

"We have been offered the opportunity to join up with some other drifters in some sort of official Alliance." I look to Gunter. "Do you want to explain?"

"Of course." He rests both arms on the table as he talks, his gaze sweeping the table. "When we began to notice, a couple years ago or so, that the OSG was making moves to … change their priorities, shall we say … we decided to make some inquiries of other ships to determine if there might be any interest in forming an alliance."

"Eyes and ears," Jens says, nodding at his cousin and then at me. His eyes flicker south again before he quickly drops his head and stares at his plate once more.

"Exactly," I say. "A small group of drifters isn't going to go after the OSG, obviously, but none of us want that anyway. We just want to be able to live our lives on the drift without someone blocking access to resources we have the right to."

"Like water," Rollo says.

"Yes. Like water. Like the ability to trade and barter with who we want without worrying about being imprisoned for dealing in contraband."

"So how does the Alliance work?" Jeffers asks. "Who's in it? Are there protocols already in place? Who's the leader?"

Gunter holds up his hand to stop the barrage of questions. "Okay, so you have many questions. That is normal, I am sure. Let me begin by saying that there is no leader. Every captain remains at the helm of his or *her* ship." He nods at me. "We take a vote on things if we are not in complete agreement, but it is rare we need to do that."

"Everyone gets along. And we trade too," Jens adds.

"Who's in the Alliance? Anyone we might know?" Baebong asks.

"You have met one of them. The DS Arcadia. The others will be introduced to you in the event you agree to join and they agree to allow you to join."

"Allow us?" I look at him, confused. "I thought we were already in."

"Well, there is this small issue of you being with the OSG…"

"Formerly with the OSG," Gus says. "Big difference."

I'm grateful for the smile he gives me and the support.

"Yes, of course, but I need to have a conversation with them to assure them it is not a problem."

"What's the mission?" Jeffers asks. "Of the Alliance, I mean."

"Our mission is simply to enable drifting as it has always been."

"And you accomplish this mission how?" Baebong leans in, more interested than I've seen him since we sat down at the table.

"We position ourselves together around resources when we are in need and act as eyes and ears for one another as we access those resources. We play a little bit of hide and seek, maybe you could say, with the OSG when necessary."

"You have a cloaking device. I'd love to get my hands on one of those," Baebong says.

"Me too," Tam says.

"All of our technology will be loaned to you, in exchange for whatever you might have to give to us of equal value." Gunter smiles, and I recognize the sly quality to it for what it is. He's not in the business of running a charity, but then again, neither am I. I can respect that.

"What about the disk?" Tam asks.

The table goes silent.

Jacov's jaw bounces out several times, but he doesn't say a word.

"We will give you a chicken for this disk you do not have," Gunter says, all traces of humor gone. "It will keep its presence masked. But you are not to reveal it to anyone without first some training and approval. Do you under-stand?" He looks right at me.

I nod. "I understand."

"So when will we know?" Lucinda asks. "Whether we're approved for membership or whatever?"

I wonder if she's asking because she needs time to de-cide if she's leaving or not, but there's no way for me to know. She's getting smarter about sharing her emotions, keeping her face almost as blank as Baebong's is.

"Tomorrow. Maybe two days. I will see. You can send me your resting coordinates, and I will contact you when I know."

I nod. "That works for me. And as far as I'm concerned, it's all I need to know right now, because I'm starving. What's for dinner?"

My crew smiles, even Lucinda, so I'm happy for once that my stomach has decided to take over the running of the show. Jeffers reaches across the table and lifts a lid from a pot in the middle. "Vegetable stew." Another dish is revealed by Lucinda. "Rice," she says. Jens holds up the rest of the rock hard loaf. "And not fresh at all bread!"

Laugher fills the room as hands reach out to grab and pass food. The meal is nothing like I used to eat in my father's home as far as quality or quantity, but it's still the best I've ever had. Today I'm breaking bread with my crew and with a possible ally in the dining room of my very own DS. As far as I'm concerned, life doesn't get any better than this.

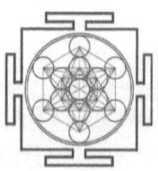

WANT MORE?

The adventures of Captain Cass and the crew of the DS Anarchy continue... For more of the humor, writing style and action you enjoyed in Book 1, find the next books in the *Drifters' Alliance* series at your local or online retailer! If you don't find the books on the shelf at your local bookstore, you can order them at the front desk.

Being an independent author, I depend entirely on *you*, the reader, to get the word out about my books. If you liked this book, won't you please leave a review online and recommend it to a friend? The more you spread the word, the more books I can write, and nothing would please me more than to put a new book in your hands every single month.

I read all my reviews!

Find more Elle Casey books at the following retailers:

Amazon
iBooks
Barnes & Noble
Google Play
Kobo
Walmart
Your Local Library via the OverDrive ebook platform

Other Books by Elle Casey

CONTEMPORARY URBAN FANTASY

War of the Fae (10-book series)
Ten Things You Should Know About Dragons
(short story, The Dragon Chronicles)
My Vampire Summer
Aces High

DYSTOPIAN

Apocalypsis (4-book series)

SCIENCE FICTION

Drifters' Alliance (ongoing series)
Winner Takes All (short story prequel to Drifters'
Alliance, Dark Beyond the Stars Anthology)
The Ivory Tower (short story standalone, Beyond the
Stars: A Planet Too Far Anthology)

ROMANCE

By Degrees
Rebel Wheels (3-book series)
Just One Night (romantic serial)
Just One Week
Love in New York (3-book series)
Shine Not Burn (2-book series)
Bourbon Street Boys (4-book series)
Desperate Measures
Mismatched

ROMANTIC SUSPENSE

*All the Glory: How Jason Bradley Went from
Hero to Zero in Ten Seconds Flat*
Don't Make Me Beautiful
Wrecked (2-book series)

PARANORMAL

Duality (2-book series)
Monkey Business (short story)
Dreampath (short story standalone,
The Telepath Chronicles)
Pocket Full of Sunshine (short story & screenplay)

Want to get an email when my next book is released?
Sign up here: www.ElleCasey.com/news

ABOUT THE AUTHOR

Elle Casey, a former attorney and teacher, is a NEW YORK
TIMES, USA TODAY, *and Amazon bestselling American author who lives in France with her husband, three kids, and a
number of horses, dogs, and cats. She has written more than 40
novels in less than 5 years and likes to say she offers fiction in
several flavors. These flavors include romance, science fiction,
urban fantasy, action adventure, suspense, and paranormal.*

A personal note from Elle ...

If you enjoyed this book, please take a moment to leave a
review on the site where you bought this book, Goodreads,
or any book blogs you participate in, and tell your friends!
I love interacting with my readers, so if you feel like shooting the breeze or talking about books or your family or
pets, please visit me. You can find me at ...

www.ElleCasey.com
www.Facebook.com/ellecaseytheauthor
www.Twitter.com/ellecasey
www.Instagram.com/ellecaseyauthor

www.ingramcontent.com/pod-product-compliance
Lightning Source LLC
Chambersburg PA
CBHW031317170626
46807CB00002B/459